He had a daughter!

He couldn't remember the bomb that had almost killed him, but he doubted its impact had been greater than the news he's just assimilated.

He was a father. Catherine Erickson had borne his child.

Stunned by the knowledge, overwhelmed by a myriad of emotions—joy, surprise, pride—he couldn't move, couldn't breathe.

You have to think like Trace Gallagher, damn you, or you'll ruin everything!

His daughter. Damn, he couldn't keep the tears from his eyes.

Hot anger flooded him suddenly and seared the tears away, and he crushed the fate that kept him from acknowledging his identity to the woman he loved more than life and to the daughter he hadn't known existed.

Dear Harlequin Intrigue Reader,

The summer is here and we've got plenty of scorching suspense and smoldering romance for your reading pleasure. Starting with a couple of your favorite Harlequin Intrigue veterans...

Patricia Rosemoor winds up the reprisal of THE McKENNA LEGACY with *Cowboy Protector*. Yet another of Moira McKenna's kin feels the force of what real love can do if you're open to it. And not to be outdone, Rebecca York celebrates a silver anniversary with the twenty-fifth title in her popular 43 LIGHT STREET series. *From the Shadows* is one more fabulous mystery coupled with a steamy romance. Prepare yourself for a super surprise ending with this one!

THE CARRADIGNES come to Harlequin Intrigue this month. *The Duke's Covert Mission* by Julie Miller is a souped-up Cinderella story that will leave you breathless for sure. This brawny duke doesn't pull up in a horse-drawn carriage. He relies on a nondescript sedan with unmarked plates instead. But I assure you he's got all the breeding of the most regal royalty when it counts.

Finally, Charlotte Douglas brings you *Montana Secrets*, an emotional secret-baby story set in the Big Sky state. I dare you not to fall head over heels in love with this hidden-identity hero.

So grab the sunblock and stuff all four titles into your beach bag.

Happy reading!

Sincerely,

Denise O'Sullivan
Associate Senior Editor
Harlequin Intrigue

MONTANA SECRETS
CHARLOTTE DOUGLAS

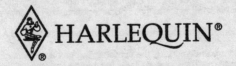

TORONTO • NEW YORK • LONDON
AMSTERDAM • PARIS • SYDNEY • HAMBURG
STOCKHOLM • ATHENS • TOKYO • MILAN • MADRID
PRAGUE • WARSAW • BUDAPEST • AUCKLAND

ISBN 0-373-22668-3

MONTANA SECRETS

Copyright © 2002 by Charlotte H. Douglas

Visit us at www.eHarlequin.com

Printed in U.S.A.

ABOUT THE AUTHOR

Charlotte Douglas has loved a good story since learning to read at the age of three. After years of teaching that love of books to her students, she now enjoys creating stories of her own. Often her books are set in one of her three favorite places: Montana, where she and her husband spent their honeymoon; the mountains of North Carolina, where they're building a summer home; or Florida, near the Gulf of Mexico on Florida's west coast, where she's lived most of her life.

Books by Charlotte Douglas

HARLEQUIN INTRIGUE
380—DREAM MAKER
434—BEN'S WIFE
482—FIRST-CLASS FATHER
515—A WOMAN OF MYSTERY
536—UNDERCOVER DAD
611—STRANGER IN HIS ARMS*
638—LICENSED TO MARRY
668—MONTANA SECRETS

HARLEQUIN AMERICAN ROMANCE
591—IT'S ABOUT TIME
623—BRINGING UP BABY
868—MONTANA MAIL-ORDER WIFE*

*Identity Swap

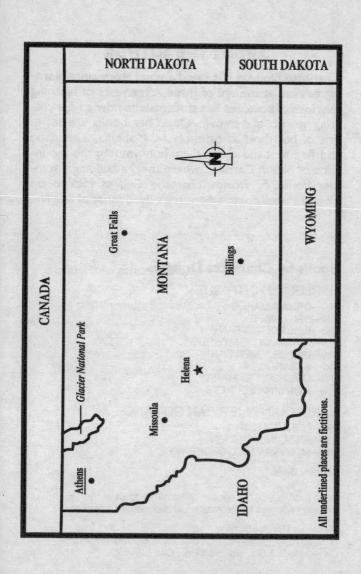

NORTH DAKOTA

SOUTH DAKOTA

CANADA

WYOMING

Great Falls

Billings

MONTANA

Glacier National Park

Helena

Missoula

Athens

IDAHO

All underlined places are fictitious.

CAST OF CHARACTERS

Ryan Christopher—A handsome and courageous marine lieutenant working undercover to fight terrorism, who loses more than his memory.

Trace Gallagher—Ryan Christopher's alter ego... and determined to protect the Eriksons at any cost.

Catherine Erickson—A pretty schoolteacher and the love of Ryan's life.

Megan Erickson—Catherine's four-year-old daughter.

Gabriel Erickson—Catherine's father.

Marc Erickson—Catherine's brother, a marine who's Ryan's best friend.

Colonel Wentworth—Head of counterterrorism at the Pentagon.

Snake Larson—Town bully and troublemaker. This time he may have committed a much more serious crime.

Derrick Hutton—Head of the terrorist group Righteous Sword, and the man responsible for too many deaths.

Dear Reader,

Montana Secrets was completed in August 2001, one month after the September 11 terrorist attacks on the World Trade Center and the Pentagon. While the story is total fiction, some elements of it are eerie predictors of what was to come—Middle Eastern terrorists launching an attack against the United States.

In addition to those sinister elements, however, this story of U.S. Marine Lieutenant Ryan Christopher and his fiancée, Catherine Erickson, contains examples of all that is best in America. When their country is threatened, both Ryan and Catherine place the safety of the nation and the protection of its freedoms above their personal safety and desires. In the end, good triumphs over evil, and, in the best Harlequin tradition, Ryan and Catherine find happiness together.

Montana Secrets is dedicated to those who lost their lives on September 11, to those at home and abroad who deter and fight terrorists who attempt to cripple our nation and destroy our freedoms, and to the courage, tenacity and union of the American people.

Sincerely,

Charlotte Douglas

Prologue

Lieutenant Ryan Christopher closed the file on his desk, rubbed his tired eyes with the heels of his palms and swiveled his chair toward the third-floor picture window of his embassy office.

Below him stretched Bahira, capital of the Middle Eastern Emirate of Tabari, white and sparkling beneath the merciless desert sun. Minarets of ancient buildings mixed with pleasant symmetry among the gleaming glass of modern skyscrapers, towering date palms and the colorful blossoms of oleander. Even in the scorching heat, the narrow cobbled streets of the bazaar teemed with traffic and pedestrians.

North of the city shimmered the endless desert, its monotonous, undulating sands dotted with oil wells that provided the tiny country's immense wealth. To the south stretched the Arabian Sea, its surface presently as calm as a single-faceted aquamarine, exactly the rich blue hue of Catherine Erickson's eyes.

Ryan smiled at the memory of the devilish sparkle in those baby blues, a quality he'd noted the first time he'd met her six years ago. Marc, his college roommate and Catherine's older brother, had invited twenty-year-old Ryan to spend the summer on their Montana ranch, and Cat, as her family called her, had been only sixteen. Like Marc, Ryan had considered the gangly teenager with a dusting of freckles across her nose and flyaway blond hair barely tamed by braids a major pest.

Young Cat had been interested in only two things—horses and spending every possible minute with her older brother, for whom she had a bad case of hero worship. Believing themselves sophisticated college men above socializing with a mere child, he and Marc had avoided her. Cat had retaliated by making Ryan's life miserable every chance she found, from leaving pebbles in his boots to short sheeting his bed.

Over the following years, Ryan had visited the ranch several times, but not until after he and Marc had graduated from officers' candidate school, received their commissions in the Marines and were on leave before their first assignment had he noticed Cat Erickson's amazing metamorphosis. The skinny teenager had been replaced by a tall, willowy young woman with luxurious blond hair, endless legs and a perfectly sculpted face whose high cheekbones recalled her Scandinavian bloodline. The only trace of the pesky kid sister remaining was the teasing gleam in her unforgettable blue eyes.

Blindsided by Cat's amazing transformation, Ryan had fallen instantly in love, aware not only of her beauty but also her wonderful qualities, which he'd either ignored or taken for granted. He'd learned to treasure her warm personality, her sense of humor, her sharp intellect and her loyalty to her family. And he'd stopped referring to her as the Pest, Marc's nickname for his sister. Instead, he had dubbed her *Kalila*, an Arabic name meaning "dearly beloved."

Now, two years after being struck by that thunderbolt, he didn't have to consult his calendar to know that in ten months, three weeks and four days his current tour of duty would end and he'd see his *Kalila* again. Not only see her, but marry her, too. When that day arrived, he'd gladly shuck the military spit-and-polish, the chain of command and the taut nerves and constant vigilance of his covert assignment to the United States Embassy in Tabari.

Ever since his childhood as an orphan running wild on the rough streets of Chicago, he'd longed for a home, yearned for a family of his own. Until a few years ago, he'd thought the Marine Corps could take the place of that family. He'd joined up with high hopes of a stellar career with a meteoric rise to the upper echelons of command.

On his last leave, however, after having fallen hard for Cat, he'd realized the military was a poor substitute for fulfilling his dreams of a home of his own. He wanted to make a life with Cat, to have a *real* family, a wife and children. Now he dreamed of his upcoming marriage and a peaceful life with Cat, running her family's ranch with his best friend and current undercover operative, Marc Erickson.

Ryan turned from the window as Marc stepped into the office from the adjoining bathroom.

Ostensibly, Ryan and Marc were assigned as translators to the contingent of Marines who guarded the embassy. In reality, they were a crack duo of counterterrorists under orders from the Pentagon to locate and identify the antinationalist terrorists who'd threatened not only the American embassy but Prince Asim Barakuh Ben Yaman, the sovereign leader of Tabari.

The translators' office, in a corner of the top floor of the embassy appeared as a simple clerical operation to anyone who entered. Only Ryan, Marc and their commanding officer, Major Barker, knew of the high-tech equipment hidden behind panels and the secret passage that allowed them unobserved and unfettered entrance to and exit from the building.

Marc had changed from his Marine uniform to the flowing robes and burnoose worn by the men of Tabari. With his skin darkly tanned by the desert sun, only his eyes, the same color as his sister's, pegged him as a foreigner. Once he'd navigated the dark tunnel to reach the street below, sunglasses would hide that flaw.

"Sneaking out to see that belly dancer you met last weekend, cowboy?" Ryan asked. "What was her name? Fatima?"

"Faridah. What a woman," Marc said with a rueful grin and lustful sigh. "And I'm tempted. But duty calls. Our suspect's on the move."

"Derrick Hutton?" Ryan raised his eyebrows in sudden interest. "How do you know?"

"Heard him telling his buddies in the cafeteria he has the afternoon off and plans to spend it shopping in the bazaar. I'm tailing him in hopes he meets his terrorist contact. If he does, we'll know for sure that Hutton's our man."

"I'll come with you and watch your back," Ryan offered.

"No, thanks. This is just routine surveillance. I'll leave you here to finish the dirty work. Your Arabic is better than mine." Marc nodded to the documents awaiting translation on Ryan's desk.

Ryan grimaced at the stack of papers, then turned to his friend. "Call me if you need me."

"Shouldn't be any problems, but I'll stay in touch." Marc grabbed his cell phone from his desk drawer, shoved it into a pocket beneath his robes and slipped through the cleverly hidden doorway.

Ryan returned to the papers on his desk. Although the embassy had a full office of translators on the second floor, he and Marc were responsible for interpreting all sensitive documents related to military or classified matters. The work before him would take the rest of the afternoon. Resigned to the drudgery, he grabbed the top sheet, an arms agreement between the United States and the Tabarian governments, and began typing an Arabic translation into his computer.

Less than an hour later, he stood and stretched, rolled the cramped muscles of his back and thought longingly of the fresh coffee always brewing in the embassy cafeteria. If he was lucky, they'd have some of those special almond cakes, too. He was halfway to his office door when the phone rang. With a curse of regret, he returned to his desk and grabbed the receiver.

"There's a bomb in the embassy!" Marc's winded voice shouted in his ear.

"You're certain?" An attack was what he and Marc had feared, had worked to prevent, but Ryan still couldn't believe their suspicions had actually materialized.

"Our suspect told his contact the explosives are in place. They'll blow any minute. Prince Asim is visiting the ambassador. Get them both to safety."

Ryan didn't argue. He and Marc had been fully briefed—the death or injury of Prince Asim would create an international crisis and strain the United States' relations with the other Arab states. "I'm on it."

"I'll call Major Barker to implement the emergency evacuation plan. I'm on my way back to the embassy now." From the jolting of Marc's voice, Ryan could tell he was on the run.

Ryan slammed the receiver into its cradle. Years of training and discipline enabled him to shove terror and visions of carnage and destruction aside. Adrenaline pumping, he sprinted for the door. He raced past the elevator into the stairwell and descended the steps three at a time.

On the ground level, he burst out of the stairway and dashed along the marble-floored hallway toward the ambassador's office. Outside the massive double doors, two uniformed Marines snapped to attention and saluted at his approach. Two strangers in dark suits and native head coverings, Asim's bodyguards, stirred uneasily at his advance.

Ryan ignored them all and slammed through the doors without knocking. The ambassador, a tall, scholarly-looking man, glanced up from behind his desk in surprise.

"Code Red, sir," Ryan announced.

The ambassador's face paled, and he shoved quickly to his feet. "Has the rest of the embassy been notified?"

"Yes, sir."

"What is happening?" Asim, obviously annoyed at the intrusion, glared at Ryan.

"No time to explain." Ryan grabbed Asim by the elbow and jerked the sovereign of Tabari from his seat. "We have to get you back to your palace immediately, Your Highness. The embassy is not safe."

With an imperious gesture, Asim shook his arm free. The prince, however, was no fool. When the ambassador rounded his desk and motioned for the prince to follow, Asim didn't hesitate. He fell immediately into step behind the ambassador, who was hurrying for the double doors.

Ryan dogged the prince's footsteps. As an afterthought, he pulled the solid wooden doors closed behind him as they left the office. If he could get the prince to his car and away from the embassy, then he could concentrate on conducting a search for the—

A massive concussion shook the building.

In the same instant, Ryan flung himself on the

prince's back, forced him to the floor and covered the sovereign's body with his own.

The huge marble tiles lifted beneath him, and the corridor exploded around him. A flash of phosphorescent fire blinded him, and collapsing rubble crashed into his back. A heavy object grazed his forehead, and the coppery taste of blood filled his mouth. Dust and smoke saturated the air, and he couldn't breathe. He attempted to rise, but a falling beam caught him between his shoulder blades and knocked him flat once more.

Won't have to look for the bomb, he thought woozily and would have laughed if his lungs hadn't hurt so badly and had held enough air. *Looks like the bomb found me.*

With every nerve ending screaming with pain, he drifted into merciful darkness.

Chapter One

Buttoning her suede jacket against the early evening chill, Catherine Erickson stepped onto the broad front porch of the ranch house and stared at the snow-capped peaks along the Montana-Canada border.

Although the air was cool, the angle of the sun hanging high above the western mountains even this late in the evening heralded the approach of summer. Wrapping her hands around a mug of hot coffee, she settled into one of the rough bark chairs, propped her boots on the porch rail and, lost in memories, gazed across the rolling upper pastures of High Valley Ranch.

She missed Ryan.

Catherine *always* missed Ryan, but somehow in summer she missed him more, when the dull, ever-present pain transformed into a sharp, unbearable ache.

Instead of focusing on the cattle feeding on the tall lush grass or, beyond them, the river swollen with melted snow, she saw in her mind's eye a tall, muscular figure striding toward her up the front walk, his mahogany-colored hair and khaki-brown eyes glinting in the sun, his broad grin accentuating the cleft in his strong, square chin, his arms open wide in greeting. His nose, broken once in a boyhood brawl, was his handsome face's only imperfection, but even that flaw added to his rakish appeal, and she had never been happier than when those strong arms closed around her and lifted her off her feet and his deep, smooth baritone voice sounded her name.

Her smile at the recollection grew wistful. He hadn't always been so glad to see her.

When Marc brought his college roommate home for the summer the year she was sixteen, Ryan had followed her brother's lead, yanked playfully at her braids and called her the Pest. Cat, on the other hand, had immediately been smitten. She'd always thought Marc hung the moon, but his handsome young friend from Chicago had been the perfect manifestation of all her adolescent fantasies. Ryan, however, seemed unaware that she existed most of the time.

Not that he was ever inconsiderate or rude. His innate good manners made him the perfect guest. He arrived with books or candy for her and a bottle of fine whiskey or a box of hand-rolled cigars for her father. And unlike Marc and her dad, who considered the kitchen women's territory, Ryan insisted on helping her with the washing up after meals.

"You don't have to do this," she'd protested that first night when he'd entered the kitchen, picked up a dish towel and begun drying the skillet she'd just scrubbed. "Marc and Dad wouldn't be caught dead in here."

"Everybody pitched in where I grew up," Ryan had said with an easy grin. "Made the work go faster."

His hand grazed hers when she passed him a pan, and the unexpected contact had sent her teenage heart into a wild flutter. She pivoted quickly toward the sink to hide her blushing cheeks.

Ryan chatted constantly as they worked, but always about the ranch. His curiosity about their way of life had seemed insatiable.

"What's a quarter horse?" he would ask, or, "How did your dad choose which breed of cattle to raise?" or, "How many head can your acreage support?"

He'd posed plenty of questions about the ranch and Montana, all right, but never any about her. Cat had soon accepted that Ryan didn't even think of her as a girl, much less a woman. When he wasn't teasing her or helping out in the kitchen, he'd treated her as if she were a fence post. Which wasn't surprising. Why should he notice her? A fence post was the ideal description of her feminine attributes. She'd never bothered with how she looked. And she'd been too tongue-tied with awe to converse wittily with their handsome visitor.

Until the summer she'd turned twenty.

Before Ryan and Marc arrived to spend their leave prior to their first overseas posting, she'd carefully

planned her campaign and laid her trap like the best
military strategist. Ryan hadn't visited the ranch in
over a year, and in that interval, Cat had learned to
show off her best features. Choosing well-cut and
properly fitted clothes instead of wearing Marc's cast-
offs made even her usual jeans and plaid shirts alluring.

With an art close to magic, Madge Kennedy down
at the Kut 'n Kurl in town had trimmed Cat's untamed
hair into an attractive shoulder-length style that
showed off her heart-shaped face to best advantage.
Adding subtle makeup, a killer sky-blue dress that
emphasized her shapely figure and matched her eyes
and sporting strappy heels that showed off long legs
formerly hidden beneath denim and boots, Cat had
paced nervously in her bedroom until Ryan's arrival.

She usually waited for her brother and Ryan on the
front porch, then ran flying down the path into Marc's
arms for a bear hug upon their arrival, but that day
she delayed, holding back until she heard them enter
the spacious living room. Then she made her entrance.

When Marc spotted her, his jaw dropped and his
eyes widened. "Who are you, and what have you
done with the Pest?" he demanded, circling her for a
closer inspection and shaking his head in amazement.

Her attention darted immediately to Ryan, who had
dropped his bag, crossed his arms over his chest and
leaned one shoulder against the doorjamb, his expression serious but his eyes shining. "Looks like
your little sister is all grown up now, cowboy."

She reveled in the obvious approval in Ryan's voice but said nothing, afraid she'd spoil the effect she'd worked so hard to create.

"Man, oh, man." Marc blinked in disbelief. "If I'd known you'd turned into such a hot number, Pest, I'd never have brought this ladykiller into the house."

"Ladykiller?" Cat experienced a moment of panic. Somehow she'd neglected to consider the possibility that Ryan already had a girlfriend. Marc had never mentioned one. Fixing her anxious gaze on Ryan, she was glad he couldn't hear her heart pounding beneath the scooped neckline of her dress. He met her glance, but his expression remained inscrutable.

"Yeah, the women are wild about him," Marc explained with the fraternal grin that made her tingle with happiness to have her brother home again. "Everywhere we go, women are always throwing themselves at him. Many a time I've had to sacrifice and place myself between him and harm's way."

"Sacrifice?" Ryan said with a wry laugh. "So that's what you call it."

Marc shrugged. "You've never seemed interested in any of the female attention. I was just trying to save you the aggravation."

Ryan stared at Cat with a laser look that heated her from head to toe. "I think," he said in a deliciously languid tone, "my interest has just been piqued."

Inwardly savoring the possibility of victory, Cat remained outwardly cool. "I'm sure plenty of girls will be happy to hear that at the dance tonight."

"What dance?" Marc asked.

"You've been away too long, brother dear," Cat said. "How could you forget the annual Territorial Celebration at the town hall?"

Marc turned to Ryan. "The music's kind of hokey, but the food's always good. Want to go?"

"If you guys are too tired," Cat said quickly, "I have a casserole I can heat for your supper before I leave."

She held her breath, waiting for their reply. She'd dreamed for months of dancing with Ryan, wondering how his arms would feel around her, dying to talk with him alone without Marc claiming all his attention.

"I don't know about you, cowboy," Ryan said, "but I think you'll be taking a chance letting Cat go alone looking like that. She'll need the Marines to keep the locals at bay."

"You could be right," Marc agreed.

Ryan nodded. "We'll have to volunteer."

Yes!

Cat called on every ounce of self-control to keep from pumping her fist in victory. Ryan had noticed her at last, but she'd have to take care not to appear too interested. If he guessed how strongly she felt about him, he'd hit the Libby highway running and never look back. The last thing she wanted was to scare him off by seeming too eager.

"Do you have a date?" Ryan asked, catching her by surprise.

Her earlier panic returned. Would he think nobody else found her interesting?

Marc jumped to her rescue. ''Nobody brings a date to the Territorial Celebration. Everyone just shows up and has a good time.''

Less than an hour later, Cat was sandwiched between Marc and Ryan on the front seat of Marc's truck, headed for town. She and Ryan each balanced one of her homemade huckleberry pies, her contribution toward the evening's covered dish dinner, on their laps. Occasionally, when the road curved, she slid toward Ryan, grazing his thigh with her own, relishing the warmth of the contact and making her even more aware of his clean, rugged, masculine scent and the attractiveness of his profile.

Telling stories of his and Marc's adventures at the Defense Language Institute where they'd studied Arabic and other Middle Eastern languages in preparation for their posting to Kuwait, Ryan kept her laughing, but her thoughts constantly strayed to the dancing that would follow supper and her hopes for spending time alone with him.

When they arrived, the town hall was bustling with people. In the adjacent tree-shaded park, tables had been erected from sawhorses and planks and covered with cloths, and tiny white lights had been strung through the trees. The tables were already loaded with food.

Cat spied her father, Gabriel, among the men circling the smoking barbecue pit. He'd left the ranch with his side of beef and gallon of secret barbecue sauce long before Marc and Ryan had arrived and was helping with the cooking. The succulent odors drifting on the breeze made her mouth water, and she was surprised to discover she was hungry. She had expected to be too excited to eat, but being near Ryan seemed to activate all her senses, even her appetite.

While Marc and Ryan crossed the park to greet her father, Cat peeked inside the open doors of the town hall, decorated with red, white and blue streamers, and watched the band setting up on the stage at the far end of the room that had been cleared for dancing. When the mayor rang the bell in the hall's squat tower, the signal for supper to begin, she returned to the park to join her family and Ryan.

Ryan sat beside her at supper, but Marc and her father monopolized the conversation with talk of the ranch and the problems created by the dry spring they'd had. Later, however, when the band in the hall began playing their first slow song, Ryan asked her to dance. Feeling as if she were walking on clouds, she accompanied him into the building and slid happily into his arms.

Even though he was dressed casually in jeans and a chambray shirt, Ryan carried himself with an unmistakable military bearing that turned the heads of every woman in the room. The charismatic confidence of a man accustomed to command blended with the fluid grace of a body trained and coordinated like a perfectly tuned machine, and he danced like a dream. Cat had to struggle to keep her mind off the delicious pressure of his hand at the small of her back. That, combined with the dangerous warmth in his eyes, made concentrating on their conversation difficult.

"Marc tells me you graduate from college next June," Ryan said. "What will you do then?"

"Teach. I'll be interning in the fall."

"Will you stay in Montana?"

"I hope to get a job at the high school here in town."

"That's a surprise."

"Why?" She drew back and gazed at him.

"I figured you had the wanderlust, like Marc. The only reason he joined the Marines was to travel."

"But as soon as he's seen the world," Cat explained, "he's heading back to help Dad run the ranch. For Marc, Montana will always be home."

"And you don't want to travel?"

"I'm a homebody. I have everything I need right here."

Except you, she thought.

"What will you teach? Elementary school?"

She shook her head, pleased at his interest. "High school history."

Ryan groaned. "I hated history in high school."

"Then you didn't have the right teacher."

His killer grin returned. "If my teacher had looked anything like you, I'm sure I would have enjoyed the class a whole lot more."

Her cheeks heated at his compliment, a reaction she couldn't control, one that she'd inherited from her mother and that caused her endless embarrassment.

"My old history teacher made us memorize long lists of people, places and dates," Ryan said. "Why did you choose such a boring subject?"

"But it isn't!"

He cocked an eyebrow skeptically. "I'll need evidence before I'll believe that claim."

She studied his face, wondering if he'd reverted to teasing her, but his expression seemed serious.

"History is much more than people, places and dates," she said. "I think the most important lesson we can learn from history is how choices always have consequences, whether those choices are made by nations or individuals."

"The old 'those who don't remember history are doomed to repeat it' theory?"

"Something like that." She glanced at him sharply, still concerned that he was making fun of her, but his eyes revealed nothing but interest. "Students need to understand the importance of cause and effect, to realize people have control over their lives, that history isn't events that happened at random. It's the result of previous decisions."

Ryan chuckled, and her heart sank. He *was* making fun of her.

"What's so funny?" she demanded.

"Not funny. Amazing. All this time I thought you didn't care about anything but horses. And here you are, a philosopher."

She scowled. "You make me sound ancient and stuffy."

He leaned back and considered her with a look that made her pulse race. His magnificent hazel eyes deepened to a hue more green than brown. "Not stuffy or ancient. Something much, much better."

Flustered by the innuendo in his words, she sought escape from his intense scrutiny. "Well, this room is definitely stuffy. Can we get some fresh air?"

"Sure."

He twirled her slowly toward the door where a cool breeze entered and alleviated the stifling heat that smothered the dance floor. When he released her, she felt suddenly bereft, until he placed his hand at the small of her back again. He steered her through the crowd that edged the dance floor and out the wide front doors.

The covered dishes had been cleared and the tables disassembled in the park, and the sun had set, leaving the area in darkness except for the faint twinkle from strings of tiny white lights.

Ryan threaded his fingers through hers and led her to a park bench in the shadow of the trees. She sat on one end, and he settled beside her.

Her plan for being alone with him had worked perfectly. She'd had her dance with Ryan, and she should be happy that they were together in this cozy, secluded spot, but all she could think of was his departure in a few days for the other side of the world.

"Why did you join the Marines?" she asked.

He leaned against the back of the bench and stretched his long legs in front of him. "I have no family. The Corps gave me a place to belong."

"No family, not even aunts or uncles?" She couldn't imagine life without her brother and father, and she was only now adjusting to her mother's death.

Even though Ingrid had been gone for several years, Cat still missed her every day.

Ryan shook his head. "No family that I know. I was abandoned on the steps of a Chicago church shortly after I was born. Father Ryan at Saint Christopher's found me. That's how I got my name."

He'd never talked about his childhood before, and his story fascinated her. "You were raised by a priest?"

Ryan laughed, a pleasant, throaty sound that echoed in the emptiness of the park. "I'd probably have turned out better if I had been. I spent the first ten years of my life in an orphanage, then bounced from one foster home to another—when I wasn't in juvenile detention."

Her heart went out to the child he'd been, orphaned, abandoned and alone. "Somehow I can't picture you as a juvenile delinquent."

"I was one tough, angry little kid, and I took out my frustrations and unhappiness on everyone and everything around me."

"But you're not like that now. What changed you?"

"Margaret Sweeney."

Cat's heart sank. There was another woman in his life after all. "How did she change you?"

"When I was twelve and already had a rap sheet as long as my arm, I went along with some older boys when they stole a car. They wrecked the car, and the cops caught us. When I went before the juvenile judge, she gave me a choice. I could go to live with

Margaret Sweeney as my foster mother or be sent to the strictest, most dreaded juvenile facility in Chicago.''

Cat was relieved to learn the woman was no rival for her. ''And you opted for Margaret Sweeney?''

He nodded. ''I'm a walking example of your choices-and-consequences theory. If I hadn't made that choice, I'd either be a lifer or dead by now. Instead, I have my whole life and a great career ahead of me.''

''What was so special about Margaret Sweeney?''

Ryan laced his fingers behind his head and gazed into the darkness as if remembering. ''She only took in the toughest cases, the boys and girls on the verge of ruining their lives forever.''

''She must have been a very strong person.''

Ryan grinned. ''That's the irony. She was a small, almost birdlike woman that a puff of wind could have blown away.''

Cat frowned. ''Then how did she handle such tough kids?''

''She loved us and believed in us with her whole heart. Most of us would rather have died than disappoint her. I lived with her for the next six years, until I went away to college—on scholarship, thanks to her.''

''She sounds like a wonderful woman. I guess you could consider her your family.''

Ryan sighed, and when he spoke again, his voice was heavy with sadness. ''If she were still alive. She died of cancer the year before I graduated. I always wished she could have seen how I turned out. More than anything, I wanted Margaret Sweeney to be proud of me.''

"I have a feeling she knows what you've done," Cat said softly, "and she is proud."

Ryan draped his arm around her shoulder and drew her closer. "You're a good listener. How come I've never noticed that before?"

"You've never really talked to me like this before." Cat's breath caught in her throat as he dipped his head toward hers, and she closed her eyes in anticipation of his kiss.

"There you are, Catherine Erickson," a coarse, slurring voice called. "I been looking all over for you."

Startled, Cat opened her eyes. Ryan withdrew his arm and glanced at the tall figure gazing down at them. The long neck of an empty beer bottle dangled between his meaty fingers. Her heart sank when she recognized Snake Larson, an old classmate of Marc's who had graduated from class bully to town menace. Tall, muscle-bound, with no neck, beady eyes and a constantly flickering tongue that had earned him his nickname, Snake was trouble personified.

"Why were you looking for me?" Cat asked, unable to keep the irritation from her voice.

"I was watching you inside," Snake said with a leer that was evident even in the darkness. "For a skinny kid, you filled out good. Come back and dance with me."

"I've had enough dancing, thank you." Cat hoped he'd take the hint and leave.

"Not until you've danced with me."

"She said no." Ryan's voice was soft but deadly. Only a fool or a drunk would have missed the threat in his tone.

Snake was both.

"Oh, yeah?" Snake said with a snarl. "We'll see about that." He lunged toward Cat.

With a move so rapid, if she'd blinked she'd have missed it, Ryan sprang off the bench and twisted Snake's arm behind his back, effectively immobilizing him.

The bully winced in pain. "Lemme go and I'll beat your ass."

"You're drunk." Ryan released the big man and pushed him away. "Go home and sleep it off."

"Nobody tells me what to do." With a fierce swing, Snake shattered the beer bottle against the nearest tree and retained the jagged top as a weapon.

Cat stifled a scream and jumped to her feet. Her first instinct was to run for help, but Snake Larson stood between her and the town hall.

"Don't worry, Cat." Ryan's voice was calm. "Stay out of the way. I'll take care of this."

Cat's heart caught in her throat. Ryan was tall, but Snake towered several inches above him and outweighed him by almost a hundred pounds. From all accounts Cat remembered, Snake also fought dirty. Plenty of men in the area bore the scars of Snake's wrath.

With a howl of rage, Snake charged Ryan. The Marine stepped deftly aside, and the bully plowed headfirst into the trunk of an ancient maple. He straightened for a moment, shook his head as if to clear it, then crumpled into a heap at the foot of the tree.

"We'd better call the paramedics," Ryan said. "He probably gave himself a concussion."

Ryan had won the fight without throwing a punch.

Cat moved to his side. While she was grateful for his physical prowess, she was sick with disappointment over the way the night had ended. She'd planned for every contingency.

Except Snake Larson.

Ryan seemed to know her thoughts. "Don't let that drunk spoil your fun. I've had a great time."

"Me, too."

Before she realized what was happening, she had found herself in Ryan's arms. His fleeting kiss had been swift and gentle but filled with promises of much more to come.

Before his leave was over, he'd made good on those promises. Later, when he'd returned from Kuwait, he'd asked her to marry him. She hadn't hesitated to agree. And although Ryan hadn't lived long enough to know it, during that last blissful leave, their daughter, Megan, had been conceived.

Cat closed her eyes and issued a silent prayer of thanks for her beautiful daughter, the unexpected blessing that had given Cat and her father a reason to endure after Ryan and Marc had died. More than a reason to endure, Cat thought. Megan was her whole life. Cat couldn't think of anything she wouldn't do for her daughter.

Ryan's daughter.

Stiff from sitting so long on the porch, Cat set aside her cold coffee and tugged her jacket closer. She'd never forget those special weeks over five years ago that she and Ryan had spent together before he left for Tabari, especially the first time they'd made love—

The whine of an engine straining on a steep grade and the clash of changing gears jerked her from her recollections, and anger flashed through her. Besides Megan, memories of Ryan were all she had, and she resented anything that interrupted her reminiscence. Pushing to her feet, she watched the unfamiliar vehicle approach.

The battered pickup pulled to a stop before the front gate, and the driver stepped out. Even in the gloom of the gathering twilight, Cat immediately recognized the huge man's threatening silhouette.

Snake Larson.

She shivered with the unearthly awareness that her trip down memory lane had conjured up the last person in the world she wanted to see.

"Hello, Snake," she called as he swaggered toward the porch. "What are you doing back from Billings? I heard you've been working a construction job down there the last few years."

He grinned, teeth gleaming yellow in the dim light.

"Job's finally finished. I've come home to work trails for the Forest Service this summer."

At the bottom of the steps, he stopped and removed his hat. His eyes, small and unpleasant, at least looked clear. He didn't act drunk, either, but with Snake, the difference between sobriety and inebriation was hard to discern. He was infamous for his volatile moods, unpredictable escapades and an amazing capacity for holding his liquor.

"Good to see you again, Cat."

"If you've come to visit Dad, I'll get him." She started toward the door.

"Don't bother," Snake called. "It's you I'm looking for."

"Why?" A sudden chill enveloped her.

"It's been five years since your fiancé was killed. Figured you might be ready to get out a bit."

She suppressed a shudder. "I don't think so."

"We can drive over to Bonner's Ferry. Have us some steaks and a few beers. Dance a bit. Kick up your heels. Surely you're ready to quit moping by now. And your daddy can baby-sit that bastard brat of yours."

His attitude was the same surly mix of arrogance, conceit and insensitivity for which he'd always been famous, and Cat struggled to rein in her flaring temper at the man's deliberate crudeness.

She forced a smile. "You've made a wasted trip. I've had supper already, and I have to work tomorrow."

Snake's fleshy face twisted in a snarl, and his

tongue flicked across his thick lips. "So, the rumors are true."

"What rumors?"

"That you're going to marry that weakling of a high school principal, Todd Brewster."

"You shouldn't believe everything you hear, Snake, nor half of what you see, as my daddy always told me."

He started up the porch steps. "Well, if you're not marrying Brewster, there's no harm in your riding over to Bonner's Ferry with me. We'll skip the steaks and cut straight to the beers and dancing."

In spite of her attempts to contain it, her anger ignited. "What part of *no* don't you understand? I'm not going anywhere with you. I have classes to teach tomorrow and papers to grade tonight."

"Damn, Cat, what's the fun of being a teacher if you can't break the rules?"

Snake lumbered across the porch toward her, and she was struck by two distinctly opposite reactions. The first was a sense of déjà vu so clear and indelible she expected Ryan to appear at any second, wrench Snake's arm behind his back and send him flying headlong off the porch. The second was the terrible realization that this time she was on her own, with her back to the porch wall and Snake Larson bearing down on her like the Great Northern Express whose tracks ran through High Valley's lower forty.

He was so close, she could smell his whiskey-laced breath. The man, unpredictable at best when sober, meaner than his deadliest namesake when drinking, apparently already had several shots under his belt. Claustrophobia closed in on her, clamping down on her lungs, making her struggle for air. She gauged her chances of making a break inside before he could grab her, and they weren't good.

Suddenly, the screen door slammed. Snake glanced toward the noise, then stopped his advance and took a few awkward steps backward.

"Evening, Mr. Erickson," Snake mumbled, with a look on his face like a kid who'd been caught with his hand in the cookie jar.

"Hello, Snake."

Her father stood in front of the door, his Winchester rifle cradled casually in the crook of his arm. Gabe's reputation for handling the weapon with extraordinary speed and accuracy was legendary throughout the county. From the suddenly respectful expression on Snake's face, Cat knew her tormentor was aware of her father's skill. Even though the tragic events of the past had left Gabriel sunken and prematurely aged, nothing had affected his proficiency with a gun.

"What do you want here, Snake?" Gabriel demanded.

Snake turned the brim of his hat in his hands, mangling its shape. "Came to ask Cat dancing."

"And what did she say?"

"Said she can't."

"Guess you'll be leaving then, won't you?"

One-handed, Gabriel cocked the lever of the rifle and pointed it toward Snake.

Snake rammed on his battered Stetson, lifted his hands in a gesture of surrender and eased off the porch and down the steps. He took the path at a trot without a backward glance, but at the gate, either his courage or his liquor kicked in, because he turned and shouted, "You ain't seen the last of me."

"Get out of here, Snake," her father warned, "before I fill your truck—and your worthless hide—full of holes."

Muttering a string of foul curses, Snake wrenched open the door of his pickup, climbed inside and started the engine. Grinding the gears, he circled the truck in the road in front of the house, knocking a section of picket fence flat in the process. With his engine screaming in protest and his tires spewing dust, he gunned down the road toward town.

Cat couldn't stop shaking, more from anger than from fright. Her father put his arm around her and led her inside.

"I made some fresh coffee," he said. "How 'bout I pour us both a cup?"

"You think he meant it?" Cat asked, following her father into the kitchen.

"About coming back?" Gabriel shook his head. "We're forty miles from town. Why would he waste his time?"

Pure, unadulterated meanness, Cat thought, but she kept her opinion to herself.

Under the bright lights of the kitchen, the heavy toll on Gabe of working the ranch alone the last five years was even more pronounced. His thick, golden hair had turned white soon after her mother died, but since the embassy bombing, her father had seemed to shrink and waste away before her eyes. The only times he laughed were when he played with his granddaughter. Cat didn't want to cause him more worry by voicing her concerns about Snake Larson.

She had no doubt that Snake would make good on his promise to return, and she intended to stay ready and remain on guard. Marc had taught her to shoot years ago. Tomorrow, she'd start target practice again.

She couldn't count on Ryan to protect her this time. A sob threatened to break loose from her throat. Ryan, unlike Snake Larson, would never be coming back to High Valley Ranch. The terrorist bomb in Tabari five years ago had made sure of that.

They hadn't even found enough of Ryan to send home to bury.

Chapter Two

At the same time Cat Erickson was having coffee in the ranch kitchen with her father, halfway around the world an infuriated Ryan Christopher burst into Colonel Barker's office at the reconstructed Tabarian embassy. He slammed the door behind him and stormed the commanding officer's desk.

"Why the hell didn't you tell me?" Ryan shouted.

Cool under fire, the colonel, every inch the military man with his buzz haircut, freshly pressed uniform, lean physique and unflappable calm, motioned his unexpected visitor toward a chair. "Have a seat, Trace, and calm down."

Ryan gripped the front edge of the desk and leaned toward the colonel, eyes flashing, face flushed with rage. "My name's not Trace, and you know it, dammit," he yelled.

"Stand down, soldier," Barker snapped with authority. "You're way out of line."

"You can't give me orders." The veins pulsed at Ryan's temples, and his knuckles turned white where they clutched the desk. "My enlistment expired four years ago. I don't have to answer to you or the Marines. But you damn well owe me an explanation.''

Barker stood and drew himself to his full height, still several inches shorter than Ryan, but what he lacked in stature, he made up for in severity. He riveted steely gray eyes on the younger man without blinking.

"Here's the way it is," he said with ruthless calm, one hand poised above the button on his intercom. "You can either sit down and talk this out quietly, or I'll have you escorted to the brig. Which is it going to be?"

Ryan struggled for self-control. His entire world had been thrown off-kilter just moments before, and he hadn't yet regained his balance. After what had just happened, he doubted he ever would. Taking a deep breath, he eased himself into the chair in front of Colonel Barker's desk.

Barker resumed his seat, but the stiffness didn't leave his posture. He eyed Ryan warily, as if his visitor were a bomb with a short fuse.

"When did your memory return?" Barker asked.

"This morning at the palace," Ryan said. "I'd just finished dressing when I banged my head against an open cabinet door. My memories came back in a rush."

Until that moment, Ryan had believed he was Trace Gallagher, an American who'd been working for over five years as a bodyguard to Prince Asim. A man who'd lost his memory when a bomb exploded while he was guarding the prince, who was visiting the American embassy.

"And everything came back?" Barker asked. "All your memories?"

Barker's tension had heightened visibly with his question, like a spring coiled too tight, and Ryan couldn't help wondering why his sudden cure from five years of amnesia would place his usually ice-cool commanding officer in such an apprehensive state.

The colonel leaned forward, seeming to hold his breath for Ryan's answer.

"No, sir, not everything. I can't remember the last few days before the bombing."

"Damn!" Barker slammed his fist on his desk.

Since threats hadn't gained him the response he wanted, Ryan decided on a new tack. Politeness.

"May I use an embassy phone, sir? When I told Prince Asim my memory had returned, he refused to let me place a call and demanded I report to you first. I have to call my fiancée."

Barker shook his head. "Sorry, Trace, you'll have to be debriefed before you can contact anyone."

"But Catherine—"

"No calls. That's final."

Ryan slumped in his chair in exasperation. Earlier, when his memory had returned, his first thought had been of Catherine Erickson, his beautiful and endearing Cat, his *Kalila* with eyes the color of Montana's big sky, hair the hue of aspen leaves in autumn and contagious laughter that made his heart sing. He'd had no contact with her since before the bombing, and he couldn't wait to hear her voice again.

Abandoned at birth, shifted from one stranger's home to another throughout his childhood, Ryan had never felt he truly belonged anywhere—until he fell in love with Cat. Her acceptance of him with all his flaws, her unfailing ability to make him laugh, the dreams and goals they had shared together made him realize that wherever Cat was, was home.

At this minute, he'd never been so homesick in his life.

"If she's waited five years," the colonel said gruffly, "she can wait a few more hours."

"*If* she's waited?" Ryan glanced sharply at the officer. "Doesn't Cat know I'm alive?"

Baxter leaned back in his chair and laced his fingers across his barrel chest. "You're not going to like what I have to say, but if you'll hear me out, you'll understand."

A premonition shivered down Ryan's backbone. He'd already suffered one severe shock this morning, learning he wasn't the man he'd thought he'd been for the past five years. What if something had happened to Cat?

"Cat's okay, isn't she?"

"As far as we know," Barker replied, "but we'll get to her later. First, tell me exactly how much you remember from before the bombing."

Ryan sat back in his chair, took a deep breath and forced himself to relax. Among his recovered memories was his awareness that Colonel Barker had his own way of operating. Ryan would have to allow events to unfold at his commanding officer's pace. As much as he wanted to know about Cat, to place that call and hear her voice, to reassure himself that she was all right, he'd have to answer Barker's questions first.

Ryan closed his eyes and tried to remember. "My last clear memory before the bombing was the day you met with Marc Erickson and me to alert us to a possible terrorist attack. You feared someone inside the embassy was in league with the terrorists and you wanted us to identify them."

"As it turned out, I was right. The attack *was* an inside job." Barker rubbed his chin thoughtfully. "That meeting was about ten days prior to the bombing. You don't remember anything after that?"

"There's a huge gap, sir. My next memories are of hospitals and doctors. But Marc can tell you everything about those missing days before the attack. You know how closely we worked together."

Barker grew ominously still. "I'm afraid Marc can't help us."

A sudden foreboding filled Ryan with dread. "Why not?"

"Erickson's dead."

Pierced with grief for his friend, Ryan sank deeper in his chair and closed his eyes, but he couldn't block out the pain. He forced himself to meet Barker's sympathetic gaze. "Killed in the bombing?"

Barker shook his head. "Assassinated."

"What?" The officer's response took Ryan by surprise, and he jerked upright.

The colonel rose from his chair with obvious effort, as if the world lay heavily on his shoulders. He circled his desk and perched on its edge in front of Ryan. "The day of the bombing Erickson was in the bazaar. He called on his cell phone to alert me to clear the building. Said he'd fill me in on the details later."

His expression grim, Barker stared past Ryan toward the windows that overlooked the desert. "We began the evacuation instantly, but we didn't have enough time to get everyone out before the bomb, already planted in the embassy, blew. It undoubtedly was an inside job. Those closest to the ambassador's office suffered the highest casualties."

Ryan nodded. He couldn't remember the event, but he'd read the news reports. Ninety-eight people had died that day, and scores had been seriously wounded.

"In the chaos that followed," Barker continued, "I temporarily forgot about Erickson, but three Marines who'd been off duty when the bomb exploded stumbled across him as they were rushing to the embassy. He was lying in a deserted alley, and he'd been shot in the back."

"So he never had a chance to tell you what he'd learned about the terrorists or how he knew about the bomb?"

"He spoke briefly to the men who found him before he lost consciousness." Barker fixed Ryan with a probing stare. "His last words were, 'Ask Ryan. He knows who did this.'"

Ryan fought to speak past the lump in his throat. "He never regained consciousness?"

"He slipped into a coma, and even though he hung on for over a year, he was never able to tell us anything more."

"And I'd lost my memory and couldn't name the traitor, either."

Barker nodded. "That's why we forged you a new identity as Trace Gallagher. Prince Asim gave you a home and a job as a bodyguard in the palace. We wanted to keep you safe until your memory returned."

"But that's crazy," Ryan said with a laugh. "I've been living openly in Bahira and wandering freely throughout the city ever since my rehabilitation from my injuries. Anyone from the embassy would recognize me immediately."

Barker's keen eyes filled with sadness. "Have you looked in the mirror since your memory returned?"

Ryan shook his head. "I haven't had time to do anything since I told Asim I'd remembered. His bodyguards rushed me here."

Barker pointed to a door off his office. "There's a mirror in the bathroom. You'd better take a look."

With trepidation, Ryan shoved to his feet and entered the bathroom. Bracing himself for an appearance maimed from injuries, he faced the mirror head-on.

A stranger stared back at him.

Not a horribly disfigured stranger as he'd feared, but definitely not the face of Ryan Christopher.

This man's cheekbones were higher and more pronounced, almost as if he had Native American ancestry. His once-broken nose had lost its characteristic bump and was straight and movie star perfect. The cleft in his chin had disappeared. Even his hair, once short and wavy, had grown out straight, fine and thick. The only familiar feature in the face was his eyes, the same greenish-brown that he remembered.

The face gazing back at him didn't belong to Ryan Christopher. It was Trace Gallagher's, the man he'd thought he was the last five years.

Shaken, he stepped into Barker's office. "What the hell happened to me?"

"Sit down." Barker's usual rough tone was filled with compassion. "You've had quite a shock."

Gratefully, Ryan sank into the chair he'd occupied earlier and ran his hands over his unfamiliar face as if searching for his old self. "Was this change on purpose?"

"Not exactly."

Ryan raised an eyebrow. "What do you mean?"

Barker sighed and scrubbed a rough hand over his short-cropped hair. "Immediately after the bombing, the triage team had given you up for dead. That's when Prince Asim stepped in and took over."

"Asim? Why?"

"You saved his life. He said if you hadn't rushed him and the ambassador from the office and closed those heavy doors behind you, he would have been killed. You were between the prince and the blast, and your body took the brunt of the explosion that otherwise would have struck Asim.''

As hard as Ryan tried, he couldn't remember any of what Barker described.

''Within minutes after the bombing,'' the colonel continued, ''the prince's driver rushed you to the trauma unit at the local hospital. Asim refused to accept the opinion of the trauma team there that you were beyond help. He flew you, attended by his personal physician, in his private jet to the best hospital in Cairo, where a crack team of emergency doctors managed to stabilize you.''

''That still doesn't explain my face.''

''The force of the explosion smashed you facedown onto the marble floor. To put it bluntly, the bones of your skull cracked like the shell of an egg thrown onto a sidewalk.''

Ryan winced. ''I don't recall the Egyptian hospital.''

''You wouldn't. You were in and out of consciousness and pumped full of painkillers. Once your condition improved, Asim had you moved to Switzerland.''

Ryan grunted with remembered discomfort. ''Switzerland I remember all too well.''

''Asim hired the best reconstructive surgeons in the world to rebuild your face.''

Ryan's frustration flared. ''If they were such experts, why don't I look like myself?''

''With a few more operations, you can have your old face back. But once we realized your memories were gone, we decided to leave you with a different appearance and new identity for your own protection. You're probably not aware of it, but even your voice is different, caused when your vocal cords were seared by the heat of the blast.''

"*We* decided to give me a new identity?'' Ryan said. "Who's *we?*''

"The head of counterterrorism at the Pentagon. He wants to nail the traitor and his terrorist friends responsible for the bombing. You're our best hope.''

Ryan felt a sudden icy chill. "What did you tell Catherine Erickson?''

As if reluctant to face him, Barker walked to the window and stood gazing at the desert glare with his hands clasped behind his back. "We told her you were dead.''

Ryan leaped to his feet. "You had no right to do that!''

Barker pivoted to face him, gray eyes flashing. "If she hadn't believed you dead, she would have been in terrible danger. The terrorists could have tried to trace you through her. Then they would have killed her, fearful you'd told her their identities.''

Ryan's already shattered world broke again. For five years, Cat had believed him dead. Had she gone on mourning, or had she managed to pick up the pieces and go on with her life? For all he knew she was married now, had children.

With someone else.

His anger at the terrorists blossomed and swelled. Losing his identity had been one thing. Losing Marc had been a horrible tragedy. Losing Cat, as well, was too high a price.

The colonel's expression softened. "I'm sorry, Trace. Telling her you died in the blast was the only way to keep both of you safe."

"Why do you keep calling me Trace? My name's Ryan."

"Ryan Christopher's a dead man."

"But I'm not—" Barker's implication suddenly hit him. "You think the terrorists are still looking for me?"

Barker shook his head. "Ryan Christopher's death was officially reported. He received several honors and commendations posthumously. There's no reason for anyone to doubt that Ryan Christopher's dead— as long as you remain Trace Gallagher."

Stunned, Ryan said nothing.

"As Trace Gallagher with Ryan Christopher's memories," Barker added, "you can be of tremendous service to your country."

"How's that, sir?"

"I've said too much already." Barker reached for his phone. "I'm booking you a seat on the next transport back to the States. There's someone at the Pentagon who wants to talk to you."

DERRICK HUTTON gazed at the crowded intersection in New York City's Little Italy, but he saw nothing of the traffic and crowds bustling below and ignored the delicious aromas of tomatoes, olive oil and cheeses drifting from the pizzerias and the street vendors. The wheels spinning in his brain took all his attention as he tried to put the pieces of the latest puzzle together. His contact in the American Embassy in Bahira had just called with an interesting and possibly disturbing tidbit of information.

Trace Gallagher, an American who'd worked for years as Prince Asim's bodyguard, who'd also been injured in the successful embassy bombing five years ago, a man Hutton had never heard of during his tenure in the embassy, had been secreted out of the country on a military transport yesterday headed for Washington, D.C.

This morning, Hutton had received a call from his Pentagon informant. Trace had been taken directly to the Pentagon upon arrival in Washington and was undergoing a series of tests and debriefings. The informant had promised to call back when he had more details.

Questions nagged at Hutton like an itch he couldn't scratch. Why the sudden Pentagon interest in a civilian like Gallagher? Was it coincidence that the man had been in the embassy when the bomb, intended to kill the prince, had detonated? According to local gossip, the prince had spared no expense to keep the man alive.

What was so special about one bodyguard out of dozens?

Why the sudden rush to return Gallagher to the States?

Hutton didn't have the answers, and not knowing placed him at loose ends.

He hated loose ends.

Odds were Gallagher's return had nothing to do with the Pentagon's ongoing attempt to locate Hutton's terrorist cell, but Hutton couldn't afford to be careless. Diligence and attention to seemingly unimportant or unrelated details had kept him alive so far. He couldn't slip up now, not with plans for the next attack almost ready for fruition.

When his informant reported in again, Hutton would learn all he could about Gallagher. If the man was a threat, Hutton would simply have him eliminated.

He allowed himself a rare smile. Death was always the best way to tie up loose ends.

THREE WEEKS after Snake Larson's unwelcome visit, Catherine Erickson gazed across the empty desks of her classroom to the windows that framed the towering Cabinet Mountains. Snow still crowned their peaks, but carpets of wild daisies edged the roadsides, and on the lower mountain slopes choke cherries, serviceberries and huckleberries were beginning to ripen.

June would be arriving in a few days. June, the time for brides and weddings, the month she would have married Ryan if he'd lived. In the last few years, summer had become a season she struggled to get through, fighting anew the pain of loss. Only her adorable Megan, Ryan's child, helped her to survive her grief.

Remembering, she glanced to the back row by the

window. The old wooden desk she'd occupied as a student, where she had carved her initials with Ryan's and circled them with a heart, had been replaced a few years ago with more modern furniture with un-yielding mica surfaces, but Cat felt the same ache, the same undeniable longing she'd experienced as a sixteen-year-old with her first crush.

No matter how hard she tried to convince herself, she couldn't come to grips with Ryan's death. Losing her brother had devastated her, but at least with Marc she'd had some closure.

God, how she hated that word.

After nursing Marc for nearly a year, watching him waste away in a coma, she'd been almost relieved when he'd died, freed of his suffering. When he'd regained consciousness briefly before his death, she'd been thankful for the opportunity she'd had to tell him she loved him, to show him baby Megan, to say good-bye.

She'd had no such time with Ryan. The first she'd heard of the catastrophe had been the arrival of the Marine officers and the chaplain to inform her and her father of Ryan's death and Marc's injuries. Maybe if she could have said goodbye, could have at least laid Ryan's body to rest in the family cemetery on the hill above the ranch, she could accept that he was gone.

As things stood now, five years after his dying, she still felt connected to him by some slim, tenuous but indestructible thread that wouldn't let go. Her stubborn heart insisted on waiting for a man her head told her would never return. But her heart refused to listen.

Like a broken video recorder, her life was stuck on pause. She couldn't move forward until she could free herself from the past. But the past wouldn't let her go.

"Catherine? Got a minute?"

She glanced up with a start to find Todd Brewster standing in front of her desk. "Sure."

The principal of Athens High was a good-looking man with the build of a college wrestling champion who had managed to keep in shape into middle age. The cuffs of his dress shirt rolled to his elbows, his loosened tie and open collar and his tousled blond hair indicated he'd had another busy day.

Smiling blue eyes in his boyish face looked at her. "You were lost in thought."

She patted a stack of papers piled neatly on the corner of her desk. "End-of-school burnout. The last exam is marked, the last grade averaged. I'm ready for vacation."

"That seems to be the general consensus around here," he said with a warm grin, reminding her how much she liked him, how well-respected he was by both students and faculty. In the three years since he'd arrived at Athens High, he'd won the admiration of the entire community—and her undying friendship.

The only problem, she thought with a sigh, was that he wanted to be more than friends.

"How about having dinner with me tonight?" he said. "We can celebrate another successful year."

"I doubt I'd be good company. I'm really tired."

He didn't press her, one of the many attributes she liked about him. "Another time then. But I want us to talk seriously soon. And I don't want Snake Larson causing you any more problems."

"How did you know about that?"

"I saw Gabriel at the café a couple weeks ago. He filled me in and asked me to keep an eye out in case Snake showed up here at school."

Cat nodded with understanding. Ever since Todd had revealed an interest in her, her usually reserved and unassuming father had decided to play match-maker, and Todd had been his willing accomplice. Her dad had loved Ryan like a son, but with Ryan and Marc both gone and Gabe not getting any younger, he worried about leaving Cat and Megan alone.

"Dad put the fear in Snake," she said with more confidence than she felt. "He's nothing but a bully. All hot air and no action."

Todd shook his head, his eyes worried. "Rumor has it he saw plenty of action in Billings. He'd have come home earlier if he hadn't been serving time for assault. Got into a brawl over a woman."

"I'll be careful. Don't worry."

"You know it's more than worry."

The warmth in his voice was unmistakable, and for the first time, Cat felt tempted to accept Todd's standing proposal of marriage. Alone, overwhelmed with responsibilities for the ranch and family, she realized Todd Brewster would make an ideal husband, a man she could always rely on, a man she could trust, a man whose company she enjoyed. Most compelling of all, he'd make a wonderful father for Megan.

But was he a man she could love?

Not as long as her heart belonged to Ryan Christopher.

"You still miss him, don't you?" Todd had an uncanny ability to read her thoughts.

Cat nodded, unable to speak past the threat of tears that often caught her unawares at the mention of Ryan.

Todd reached for her hand and squeezed it gently. "He was your first love. You'll always miss him. But you have to move on."

"I know." She blinked back the tears and forced a smile. "Can I take a rain check on that dinner?"

"You bet. Just name the date. I'll see you tomorrow night at graduation."

He gave her hand another gentle squeeze and left the room.

With the same nostalgia she experienced at the end of every school year, especially when she thought of her seniors, who wouldn't be returning in the fall, Cat went through her checklist. She'd marked her students' final grades on the standard computer forms, completed her textbook inventory and supplies requisitions for the fall semester, cleaned the ancient slate blackboards with lemon oil and cleared the top of her desk. All that remained was to straighten the rows of desks and close the tall windows.

Starting at the back of the classroom, she had shut

half of them when she heard footsteps at her door. At first, she thought Todd had returned, but the figure backlit by the hall windows was too tall for the principal. Her pulse stuttered when she feared for an instant the tall man might be Snake Larson.

Then she recognized the broad shoulders and slender hips of the dark silhouette, a figure etched indelibly on her mind and heart, and she grabbed the nearest desk to keep her knees from buckling beneath her.

Dizzy with hope, joy and disbelief, she finally found her voice.

"Ryan? Is that you?"

Chapter Three

Kalila.

Ryan gritted his teeth to keep from speaking his special name for her aloud and stepped into the artificial brightness of the classroom's fluorescent fixtures.

As he did, the hope and joy lighting Cat's face dulled suddenly to disappointment. When she'd called his name in recognition, relief had flooded through him. She had known who he was, so keeping his identity secret was out of his hands. As he saw it, he had no choice but to let her know he was really Ryan.

His own mirror, however, should have made him realize what her face told him now.

She was looking at a total stranger.

Struggling to hide his emotion, he felt ripped between duty and desire. He couldn't react, couldn't show her how wildly happy he was to see her again, couldn't sweep her into his arms and tell her how much he still loved her, how much he'd missed her, how sorry he was about Marc's death. How concerned he was for her safety.

No, he had to think of himself as Trace Gallagher or he'd blunder and give everything away. One slip could prove fatal not only to him but to Catherine, as well. He had to *be* Trace Gallagher in every respect, act the part to the nth degree for his mission to succeed. Having to treat the woman he loved with remote politeness galled him, but he had no choice. Failure was unacceptable, because failure meant Marc Erickson's killer and the terrorists who had murdered ninety-eight others would go unpunished, and he would be placing Cat's life in danger.

Drawing on all his military discipline to tamp down the emotions that threatened to overwhelm him, resisting with every fiber of his being the desire to rush to her and hold her close, assuming a detachment he didn't feel, he stepped into the classroom.

"Miss Erickson?"

Confusion replaced the disappointment in her summery blue eyes, but even wearing a puzzled expression, she was more breathtakingly attractive than ever. She'd matured in the last five years, at twenty-seven looking less like the ponytailed teenager he'd first met and even more like a woman than the person he'd last seen at twenty-two. An irresistibly alluring woman. Her underlying air of sadness and loss etched her face with character and lent her an aura of mystery and gravity that made her even more desirable.

He silently cursed his fate. She should have been his wife, and he had to treat her like a stranger.

"I'm Catherine Erickson." She sank onto the nearest desk and clasped trembling hands in front of her.

"Forgive me if I seem a bit shaken. I mistook you for someone else. A trick of the light, I guess."

Shoving his hands into the pockets of his slacks to keep from reaching for her, Trace moved closer. "Sorry if I startled you. I passed your principal in the hall, and he told me which room was yours."

Cat took a deep breath in an obvious attempt to regain her self-control and peered at him, a bloom of pale rose slowly returning to her cheeks after the pallor of her initial scare. Curiosity sparked in her remarkable eyes. "Who are you and why are you looking for me?"

Trace suppressed a smile. Cat was so like he remembered her, direct and to the point. He'd always known exactly where he stood with her because she'd never played the coy games some women seemed so fond of. And she'd never been afraid to ask straightforward questions.

"I'm Trace Gallagher. I just returned to the States a few weeks ago from an extended tour of duty in Tabari."

Her face paled again when he named the Middle Eastern nation, so he hastened the rest of his explanation. "I was good friends with Marc and Ryan."

Cat's eyes narrowed. "I don't remember either of them mentioning you."

"They wouldn't have. I was on assignment for military intelligence, working as a bodyguard for Prince Asim. Since Marc and Ryan were working undercover, too—"

"No one was supposed to know that." Her eyes

had widened with alarm, and he hastened to reassure her.

"As members of the intelligence community, we shared information. I kept them informed of what happened at the palace. They kept me abreast of what went on in the embassy."

Skepticism was evident in the slant of her lips, the glint in her eyes.

"Look, I don't expect you to take my word for this." He dug into his pocket, pulled out an envelope and handed it to her. "Here's a letter of introduction from Colonel Barker at the embassy—"

"Colonel?" Cat took the envelope and pulled out the letter written on official embassy stationery. Her dubious expression disappeared. "So the major's been promoted. I'm glad. Marc and Ryan both thought a lot of him, and he was especially kind to Dad and me...after."

She read the letter quickly, inserted it in its envelope and handed it back to him. "Looks like you're who you say you are, Mr. Gallagher."

He repressed a flinch at the ironic error of her words. "Call me Trace."

At that instant, Cat gazed past him to the door, and Trace turned to find the principal he'd met earlier in the hall standing in the doorway.

"Everything okay in here, Catherine?" the man asked.

"I'm fine," Cat said.

"You're sure?" the principal persisted with a proprietary air that told Trace the boss considered Cat more than just another teacher.

"Trace is an old friend of Marc's," Cat explained. "He's stopped in for a visit."

The principal looked wary. "I'll be around for a while. Buzz me on the intercom if you need me."

Catherine smiled warmly at the man. "Thanks for looking out for me, Todd. I'll talk to you later."

"Good friend?" Trace fought back a pang of jealousy.

"The best," Cat admitted. "I don't know what I'd have done without him the last few years."

Trace crushed his irrational anger against a man who had been there when he couldn't be and tried to be grateful that Cat had had friends looking after her.

Cat's expression sobered. "You still haven't told me why you're here in Athens."

"Intelligence work is a stressful job, so my handlers decided I'm due for R&R. Marc and Ryan always talked about this corner of Montana as if it were God's country. Since I've never been West, I decided to see for myself."

"You're on vacation?"

"A much-needed holiday," he said with feeling.

His statement wasn't intended as a deception. A vacation was exactly what the Pentagon had dubbed his Montana trip, even though he was on assignment.

Shortly after he had confronted Colonel Barker at the embassy, Ryan had been hustled out of Tabari aboard a military transport. Upon his arrival in the United States, a Pentagon limousine whisked him away from Andrews Air Force Base and delivered him into the hands of Colonel David Wentworth, head of counterterrorism.

After Ryan had been poked, prodded and thoroughly examined by every specialist in the medical profession from internists to psychiatrists, he'd been closeted with Colonel Wentworth for debriefing.

"You can't hold me here," Ryan protested. "My enlistment's up. I want to go home to my fiancée."

Wentworth, a heavyset man in his forties with bulldog cheeks and the proverbial fireplug physique, leaned back in his seat, steepled his fingers beneath his chin and stared at Ryan across his desk. "Of the ninety-eight people killed in the Tabarian embassy bombing, twenty-four were Marines. Twenty-five, if you count Lieutenant Erickson."

"I'm aware of that, sir."

"Are you also aware this same terrorist cell is still active in the Middle East? Or that they've recently made threats against targets here on the U.S. mainland?"

Ryan shifted uncomfortably in his chair. "No, sir."

"Righteous Sword."

"Sir?"

"That's what they call themselves, the group that claimed credit for the bombing in Tabari." Wentworth leaned forward, eyes blazing. "We need you to *remember,* lieutenant. You're our best hope of identifying and locating these bastards. In the years since the bombing, every lead has fizzled out. Tracking this group had been like chasing mist, and we're no closer to rounding them up now than we were then.''

"I want to remember, sir.'' His assertion couldn't have been more earnest. He wanted Marc's killers brought to justice and he wanted to put the military behind him and go home to Cat.

If she'd still have him.

Flipping through a thick file on his desk, Wentworth nodded. "Your psychiatric evaluations indicate your selective amnesia may be the result of the severe physical and emotional trauma you suffered when the embassy was bombed. Your mind's not ready yet to relive that horror.''

"They tried hypnosis. It didn't help.''

The colonel nodded. "That's in the file. The doctors do, however, believe there may be a possible cure.''

"Surgery?'' He'd had his fill of hospitals and didn't relish more operations, but if surgery would get him home to Cat sooner, he'd jump at the chance.

For the first time in the interview, Wentworth smiled. "The cure they suggest is much more pleasant. The doctors want you to go home, spend several weeks in familiar and comfortable surroundings. They're hopeful the experience will unlock your repressed memories.''

"I have no home to go to. I grew up in foster homes. The Corps has been my family.''

Wentworth shook his head. "We want you to go to Montana. Visit with the Ericksons. The doctors think being around your fiancée and that ranch you're so fond of might jog those critical memories loose."

Ryan grinned like a condemned man just granted a reprieve. "I wouldn't object to that, sir."

"There are certain conditions, of course," Wentworth added with a scowl. "You have to maintain your identity as Trace Gallagher."

"I can't tell my own fiancée who I am? You expect me to remember under that kind of stress?"

"Think, damn you," Wentworth snapped. "You're as intelligent an operative as I've ever had, but you're letting your emotions interfere with your brain. Those terrorists are fanatics, killers willing to blow themselves up if their deaths serve their cause. If they catch wind of the fact that Ryan Christopher, the man who knows their identity, is still alive, do you think anything will stop them from tracking you down? If you return to Montana as Ryan Christopher, they'll find you there. And if they kill you, they'll think nothing of wiping out the rest of the Erickson family while they're at it."

"Then I shouldn't go to Montana at all," Ryan said. "I don't want to endanger Cat or her father."

"We need you in Montana," Wentworth said.

"Why?" Ryan's blood suddenly ran cold. "You don't think the terrorists are after the Ericksons?"

Wentworth shook his head. "No, but we believe the Ericksons may have information that could help our investigation."

"Marc would never have breached security by telling his family classified secrets."

"Not the Marc you knew," Wentworth said, not unkindly. "But when Marc was shot and didn't resume consciousness, his family had him transferred home to care for him. It's possible, even though he was in a coma until he died, he may have muttered something—"

"Something that would have seemed like gibberish to them but that I would understand? That seems highly unlikely."

"I know we're grasping at straws, but we're desperate. We can't let these terrorists succeed again. I want to break Righteous Sword across my knee."

Reluctantly, Ryan had agreed to Wentworth's plan.

The more time Ryan had had to recover from the shock of his five-year amnesia, the more his thoughts and emotions had crystallized. As much as his personal feelings led him in the opposite direction, he realized where his duty lay. In the week following his interview with Wentworth, bringing the terrorists, especially the traitor from within the embassy, to justice had become not just a goal, but an obsession. Their capture would serve three purposes—punishment for the killers, protection at home and abroad from future terrorist attacks and, most appealing of all, freedom to return to Cat as the Ryan she remembered.

Wentworth had developed a deep background cover for Trace Gallagher, and within a week Trace was on a transport flight to Great Falls. From there, he'd caught a bus to Athens, and upon arriving in the tiny northwest Montana town, he'd come straight to Cat's school.

Even now he found it hard to believe she was standing there within arm's reach.

"Where are you staying?" Cat asked.

Trace shrugged. "Haven't had a chance to look around. Can you recommend a place?"

"There's the motel out on the highway. That's about it, unless you go into Libby or Bonner's Ferry."

"Where can I rent a car?" Unless the town had grown by leaps and bounds in the last few years, he knew the answer, but he had to play the part of the unknowing newcomer.

"Not in Athens," Cat said. "Look, I know my father will want to talk with you. He cherishes any memories he can glean of Marc. And Ryan, too. He thought of him as his second son. Why don't you come home with me, have dinner with us and spend the night? We can rustle you up some lodgings and a vehicle tomorrow."

"I don't want to impose." Trace crushed down his emotions, determined not to appear too eager. "I could always hitchhike into Libby and find a place."

"Impose?" Cat laughed, a pleasing sound like silver coins tossed on water. "Dad will be terribly disappointed if I don't bring you home."

Trace returned her smile. Securing an invitation to stay at High Valley Ranch had been too easy.

And the hardest thing he'd ever done.

CAT WAS GLAD her hands had steadied enough for her to lock the door of her classroom behind her. As startled as she'd been at Trace Gallagher's appearance, she was amazed she hadn't fainted from shock.

For that first brief instant when he had stood silhouetted in the door of her classroom, she had been positive beyond doubt that he was Ryan, even though the dreadful reality of Ryan's death contradicted her. For a brief, shining moment, she'd been willing to believe, daring to hope that Ryan had returned from the dead.

When Trace had stepped into the light, however, she'd immediately realized the absurdity of her expectations. Too much grief had made her crazy. While Trace was about the same height and weight Ryan had been, the similarities ended there. Trace's cheekbones were higher and more defined, his perfect Roman nose lacked Ryan's endearing bump, a souvenir from a boyhood rumble, and Trace's strong, square chin didn't sport Ryan's characteristic cleft. No, the stranger was nothing like Ryan.

Except for his eyes.

Stunned by the cruel fate that had placed Ryan's khaki-brown eyes in another man's face, Cat had barely been able to look at him face-to-face. Even his long, thick lashes the color of soot and the searing intensity of his gaze were the same as Ryan's had been.

Silently chastising herself for foolishly believing even for a second that Ryan had been miraculously resurrected, she had at first barely registered Trace's introduction. Only Todd Brewster's reassuring appearance at her classroom door had rooted her in reality again. But that calm had been short-lived. She tried to get her breathing back to normal and her nerves composed.

She looked forward to hearing Trace's account of Marc and Ryan's sojourn in Tabari. Any information she could learn about their last days on earth would be treasured, but she was surprised to realize she was also eager to learn more about Trace Gallagher. Perhaps it was his faint resemblance to Ryan that created the electricity between them she couldn't deny.

For the first time since Ryan's death, she was experiencing the stirrings of longing, the genuine flickers of interest in a man. She'd been close friends with Todd Brewster and found his company pleasant, but he was like a kind and gentle older brother. She'd never wondered what his arms would feel like around her, how his lips would taste. Trace's sudden appearance and faint resemblance to Ryan must have scrambled her brain, because those were exactly the questions roiling in her mind about a perfect stranger.

She took a deep breath and promised herself she'd be fine as long as she avoided a head-on confrontation with those greenish-brown eyes so like Ryan's.

And her daughter's.

She attempted to shake off the fluttery feeling the man's presence triggered. The only other time in her life she'd been so immediately attracted to a man was the first time she'd met Ryan. She doubted lightning would strike twice in her lifetime. She would have to rein in her rebellious senses or she'd make a fool of herself for sure.

Apparently unaware of the turmoil he'd generated in her, Trace leaned down beside the door and lifted a duffel bag from the floor where he'd left it.

"Is that all your luggage?" she asked.

Trace nodded. "I travel light."

She eyed the cotton sports shirt, lightweight windbreaker, casual slacks and deck shoes he was wearing, all a perfect fit and obviously good quality but more suitable for a Cape Cod weekend than a Montana summer. "Did you bring warmer clothes? The weather turns cold here, even in summer."

"Didn't have to worry about keeping warm in Tabari. Just the opposite." He fell in step beside her, shortening his stride to accommodate hers, the clatter of their shoes echoing on the hardwood floors of the empty halls.

"We've had snow flurries in June before," Cat explained, "and heat waves from the chinook winds. You never know what to expect."

She was babbling, but she couldn't help it. Her heightened awareness of the handsome man at her side had affected her brain.

"Is there a place in town that sells clothes?" he asked.

"Hayes Mercantile. It's right by the supermarket, and I have to make a stop there anyway."

"I'm just a city boy. Maybe you can help me choose what I'll need—if it's not too much trouble." He depressed the panic bar on the large double door and held the door open for her to exit the building.

"No trouble," she lied as they crossed the parking

lot to her Cherokee SUV. "I used to shop for Ryan and Marc all the time."

The last thing she needed was the intimate task of helping the enticing stranger select clothes. She'd point him in the right direction and retreat to the market.

She unlocked the rear gate of the car, and he swung his bag inside. In a few minutes they were leaving the school for the short drive to downtown, a two-block stretch of road filled with Athens's only businesses, the supermarket, Hayes Mercantile, the café, a laundromat, a service station and three saloons.

Cat, however, wasn't concentrating on the familiar landscape. All she could think of was Trace Gallagher's attractive profile and the tantalizing scent of him, uniquely masculine, a musky mix of soap, fresh air and sunshine, that teased her nostrils.

She tightened her hands on the steering wheel and silently ordered herself to get a grip on her feelings. She was no hormone-driven teenager, but a twenty-seven-year-old woman, a professional who managed crises every day in her teaching position, the mother of an active and intelligent four-year-old. Surely she could handle one handsome stranger without acting like a fool.

"Not exactly a booming metropolis," she said as she pulled into a diagonal parking space in front of the market. "It hasn't changed in my lifetime."

"I like it." Trace glanced up and down the street with interest. "With the boardwalks and the old train station, I feel like I'm really in the Old West."

She slid from the car and pointed toward Hayes Mercantile to her left. "You'll feel a lot more at home once we get you out of those city slicker clothes. I bet you grew up in a big city, didn't you?"

He hesitated only a second before answering, but long enough for her to notice and wonder whether he didn't like talking about his past.

"Syracuse, New York," he finally admitted. "Before they died my mother and father were professors at the university there."

He was either avoiding her eyes or rubbernecking to take in the few sights of the town. Either way, he evaded her gaze. That suited her just fine. The less personal their conversation, the better.

"Ever ridden a horse?" she asked.

"Not until I went to Tabari. The prince had a stable of the most magnificent Arabians in the country. He expected me to ride with him and his other body-guards, so I had to learn fast."

Cat squashed the enchanting image of Trace galloping across the desert sands dressed like an Arab sheikh. She pushed open the door of the department store and entered.

"It's good you learned. Dad will enjoy showing you the ranch on horseback," she said over her shoulder to Trace, who followed close in her wake. "You'll need jeans—Wranglers for riding—and some decent boots."

Blinking against the sting of dye gases from the dry goods that assaulted her nose and eyes, Cat approached George Hayes, the fiftyish proprietor, who was stacking flannel shirts in clear plastic wrappers beneath a Sale sign on the front counter. "Brought you a customer, Mr. Hayes."

The tall, skinny salesman, tape measure fluttering around his scrawny neck, turned and considered her from behind thick-rimmed glasses. "Howdy, Catherine. What can I do for you this afternoon?"

She jerked her thumb toward Trace. "Mr. Gallagher is visiting from out of town. He needs appropriate clothes for the ranch."

"Jeans, shirts, boots and a hat," Trace said. "And a jacket."

As if assessing sizes, Hayes gave Trace a head-to-toe appraisal. When Cat found herself engaging in the same activity and enjoying it, she diverted her eyes.

"You're in good hands with Mr. Hayes," she told Trace. "I'll do my shopping and meet you at the car."

She pivoted quickly and left the store.

What was the matter with her?

She'd assured herself earlier that she wasn't a hormone-driven teenager, but that's exactly how she'd felt, feasting on Trace's muscular good looks as if he were a teen idol. She hurried into the air-conditioned chill of the market and welcomed the aromas of everything from cantaloupes to coffee beans that drove his provocative scent away.

Hettie Merkle, who'd worked as a cashier as long as Cat could remember, lifted her head from a *Soap Opera Digest* at Cat's entry.

"Saw you pull up earlier." Hettie moved her chewing gum to her cheek to speak. "Got a new boy-friend?"

Athens was a small town where everyone knew everyone else's business, and Hettie Merkle's main goal in life was to keep the lines of communication flowing.

"He's an old friend of Marc's in town for a visit," Cat explained. "I'm taking him out to see Dad."

"Glad to hear it, honey." Hettie set her magazine aside and swiped at her henna-colored bangs with red-tipped nails. "Wouldn't want to make Todd Brewster jealous now, would you?"

"Why should he be jealous?" Cat asked with pre-tended innocence, although she was well aware half the town expected her to marry the high school prin-cipal.

"My sentiments, exactly," Hettie replied, missing the point.

Shaking her head at the woman's density, Cat headed for the produce section. She hadn't planned on company for dinner, and, not knowing Trace's taste in food, she decided to fix spaghetti with a tossed salad and garlic bread. She couldn't think of anyone who didn't like spaghetti. It was always Me-gan's first choice. For dessert, she'd make a rasp-berry-rhubarb pie.

Ryan's favorite.

The thought skewered her like a serrated blade, and she wondered if she'd ever reach a time in her life when unexpected memories of Ryan would stop hurt-ing and become only pleasing recollections.

Janet Livingston, mother of the senior class vale-dictorian, cornered Cat while she was picking through tomatoes, and Cat had to endure a detailed preview of a planned after-graduation party before she could escape to the checkout line.

When Cat stepped out of the grocery store, a tall, lean cowboy was leaning on the front fender of her SUV, boots crossed at the ankles, arms folded across his chest and a Stetson pulled low, hiding his face. Handsome and mysterious was the description that leaped to her mind. She took a moment to realize she was looking at Trace Gallagher, transformed from preppy to Western by George Hayes's sartorial magic.

"You look like one of the locals," she greeted him.

He shoved back the brim of his hat with an index finger and caught her head-on with those hazel eyes. "Should I take that as a compliment?"

"Absolutely. Nothing worse than a dude who sticks out like a sore thumb."

His lips curved in a smile that almost dimpled his cheeks, and his eyes—Ryan's eyes—flickered with good humor. "So I'm no dude?"

"Not in the greenhorn sense, no. But my students in their mangled slang version of the English language might call you *dude* and mean something else entirely." She was babbling again, but she couldn't help it. If anything, Trace Gallagher looked even more appealing in his Western duds than he had when she first met him.

"The new jeans are a bit stiff," he noted, "the shirt's creased where it was folded, and the boots need some breaking in, but overall I think I could get used to dressing this way.''

"What did you wear when you worked for the prince?'' He helped her stow the groceries in the back of the car, and she headed for the driver's side. "Flowing robes and headdresses?''

"Armani suits.'' Trace slid into the passenger seat next to her. "The prince had an image to uphold, so he provided his bodyguards with very generous clothing allowances.''

She started the engine and backed onto the street. "Living in a palace must have been a heady experience, surrounded by all that luxury.''

"I'd trade luxury for home any day.'' The longing in his voice was unmistakable.

She felt a pang of sympathy for him. He'd lost both his parents. At least she still had Gabriel and Megan. Her sympathy dissolved quickly into happiness. She was approaching the best part of her day—picking up her daughter from the baby-sitter's.

"I hope you don't mind,'' she said, "but I have one last stop to make before we head to the ranch.''

"Mind?'' He shook his head. "It's your car and your schedule. I'm just along for the ride.''

"It won't take long,'' she promised.

She turned onto a street lined with cottonwoods and pulled to the curb in front of a small white house with green shutters and a picket fence. She barely had time to turn off the ignition before the front door flew open.

Cat's spirits soared as Megan came flying down the

walkway, her legs—still pudgy with baby fat in spite of her four years—pumping hard, her golden-blond curls bouncing, her hazel eyes shining. "Mommy, Mommy, you're late!"

"Who's that?" Trace asked in a strangled tone.

"That's Megan." Cat's heart swelled with maternal pride. "My little girl."

"I didn't know," he said in the same strange voice.

Her joy at the sight of her baby was tempered with sadness. "One of my biggest regrets is that Ryan never knew he had a daughter."

Chapter Four

He had a daughter!

He couldn't remember the bomb that had almost killed him, but he doubted its impact had been greater than the news he'd just assimilated.

He was a father.

Catherine Erickson had borne his child.

Stunned by the knowledge, overwhelmed by myriad emotions—joy, surprise, pride—he couldn't move, couldn't breathe. He was glad Cat had rushed from the car to greet the little girl. Her departure had given him a moment to pull himself together. But he was going to need more than a moment to recover from this shock.

You have to think like Trace Gallagher, damn you, or you'll ruin everything!

Breathing deeply in an attempt to settle his shattered equilibrium, he concentrated on his other persona. What would Trace's reaction be to Cat's bombshell? Mild interest? A touch of sadness for Ryan's loss? He gripped the knees of his jeans with white-knuckled fingers.

Trace's hands wouldn't be shaking like leaves in an autumn breeze, that was certain.

Unaware of the chaos she'd introduced into his life, Cat released Megan and was walking toward the house with her daughter.

His daughter.

Damn, he couldn't keep the tears from his eyes.

Hot anger flooded him suddenly and seared the tears away, and he cursed the fate that kept him from acknowledging his identity to the woman he loved more than life and the daughter he hadn't known existed. Unfortunately, keeping his identity secret was more important than ever. If he told the Ericksons he was really Ryan, not only Cat and her father would be in mortal danger, but Megan, too.

His family was safe only so long as everyone, Cat and terrorists alike, believed Ryan Christopher was dead.

Pulling himself together, he watched Cat and the little girl—his little girl—approach. Cat had Megan by one hand, and in the other was a shopping bag overflowing with a small faded quilt, a well-worn teddy bear and an assortment of toys and other items.

Excitement evident in every step and an animated look on her face, the little girl bounced when she walked, keeping up a steady stream of chatter that he couldn't make out through the closed windows of the car.

Unable to take his eyes off his daughter, he burned her image in his mind. Wearing overalls, a long-sleeved pink T-shirt embroidered with bunny rabbits and edged with lace and sporting matching pink sneakers, she smiled at her mother, her round cheeks flushed with color.

Megan had *his* eyes, he realized with a start, and the same dimple that had once graced his chin. Even her hair was the same shade and texture his had been in childhood.

A dangerous lump formed in his throat. How the hell was he supposed to act as naturally as a stranger would have when the first sight of his daughter choked him up so badly he couldn't speak?

Cat circled the car, tossed the shopping bag on the back seat and lifted Megan in her arms by Trace's door. He rolled down the window. Having his own eyes stare back at him from a child's face was disconcerting.

"Megan, this is Mr. Gallagher."

The girl hid her face in her mother's neck, then peeked shyly at him with one eye. With a heart-shaped face evident beneath her baby fat, proof that she'd inherited her mother's delicate bone structure, Megan was even more adorable close up than from a distance. His arms ached to hold her.

He struggled to swallow against the boulder in his windpipe. "Hi, Megan."

"Can you say hello?" Cat prodded. "Mr. Gallagher's coming home with us tonight."

Megan turned her head just enough to expose her other eye. "Are you a teacher like Mommy?" she asked.

"No." Trace chuckled. The little minx was batting her eyelids, flirting with him!

"What are you?" Megan demanded.

I'm your daddy. "I'm a Marine."

She lifted her head and gazed at him with new interest. "Like my daddy and Uncle Marc?"

Cat, a wistful smile playing across her remarkable face, watched their exchange.

"That's right," he said.

"Uh-uh." Megan shook her head vigorously. "Wrong clothes."

"She's used to the pictures of Ryan and Marc in uniform," Cat explained.

"I have a uniform, but these aren't my working clothes," Trace said. "These are my play clothes."

"Big people don't play," Megan insisted.

"Sure they do." The longer he talked with her and watched the mischief dancing in her eyes, the more he could feel himself melting into a blob of Silly Putty that she could wrap around her pudgy little fingers. "I'm taking a vacation. That's why I came to Montana."

"You're going to come play at our house?"

"That's enough questions, young lady." Cat opened the back door, hoisted Megan into her carrier and fastened her seat belt. "You want your teddy?"

"Yes, please."

Trace could hear Cat rummaging in the shopping bag. Then the back door slammed, and she circled the car and climbed behind the wheel. He had to steel his muscles to keep from swiveling in his seat to stare at his daughter.

"Megan usually takes a nap on the way home."

"Is it far?" He knew the answer. He could follow the route blindfolded.

"Forty miles," Cat said, "but that's not considered much by Montana standards."

She turned west onto the highway, passed the district ranger station, then turned north on a secondary road that hugged the sides of steep mountains as the road climbed through thick forests of ponderosa pines and Douglas firs. Tall thistles and bushes heavy with black caps grew wild along the shoulders.

Remembering his reactions the first time he'd traveled this road, he decided he should play tourist, as a true stranger would. "You really have a ranch up here? It's nothing but mountains and ravines."

"For now."

Cat flashed him a smile. That look, mixed with the scent of her light honeysuckle fragrance, made his insides quiver with want and remembered passion. He'd known being close to her without being able to touch her would be difficult, but he hadn't imagined the brutal toll it would take on him. He felt as if he'd been squashed flat by an M-60 tank, then trampled by a platoon of raw recruits in combat boots.

"Soon," she added, "we'll reach an alpine valley that runs for miles, even across the Canadian border."

"Hence the name High Valley Ranch?"

"You got it."

He rode in silence for the next several miles, admiring the scenery, wishing his homecoming could have been more honest. The soft breathing of Megan in the seat behind him intruded on his thoughts and formed a thousand questions in his mind. Foremost was why Catherine had never told him she was expecting a child.

"Ryan never knew you were expecting?" he asked, at the risk of seeming nosy. He needed to know why she'd kept her pregnancy secret.

Without taking her eyes from the road, Cat shook her head. "I didn't know myself until a few days before the embassy bombing."

With an almost surreal vividness, he recalled their lovemaking the day before he'd left for Tabari. He and Cat had taken a picnic into the woods above the high meadow. In a secluded forest glade, throughout the long afternoon, they'd made love on a blanket spread over boughs of thick ferns and evergreens. With unforgettable recall, he could almost feel the silkiness of her skin beneath his fingers, her slight weight against the length of him. Hear the beating of her heart beneath his cheek and the soft, sweet intake of her breath when she gasped with pleasure....

He'd used protection. He'd always insisted on it until they were married, but the fact, drilled into him with a vengeance by his foster mother, Margaret Sweeney, when he was still a teenager, that only abstinence was one hundred percent effective, came back to haunt him.

"I was composing a letter," she said softly, "to

share the news with Ryan when we got word of his death.''

The heartache in her voice made him long to reach for her, and he cursed the circumstances that prevented him from telling her the truth and ending her pain.

''That must have been a really tough time.'' The steadiness in his voice, reflecting none of the turmoil within him, amazed him.

Her face soft with love, she glanced at Megan in the rearview mirror. ''Knowing I was pregnant with Ryan's child kept me going. At least I had some part of him left. Megan was born three months before Marc died. She saved Dad's life, too. He took Marc's death hard, but having a granddaughter helped ease the blow.''

''She's a beautiful child.'' He hoped she'd mistake the pride in his words for simple admiration. ''Seems smart, too.''

''Luckily, she takes after her father in looks and brains.''

''From what Ryan told me, you're no slouch in the brains department yourself, and Megan has your bone structure.'' His light, bantering tone revealed nothing of the tangle of emotions knotted inside him.

''Ryan talked about me?'' Cat seemed pleased.

''Not much.''

''Oh.'' Her voice rang with disappointment.

Trace hurried to correct her misconception. ''He didn't like how some of the guys blabbed about their girls. The way they talked about their sex lives was degrading to the women they'd been with. When Ryan spoke of you, it was always with the greatest respect.''

The blush he remembered so vividly reddened her cheeks. "What did he say?"

"That he was lucky to be engaged to the prettiest, smartest, most fun-to-be-with woman he'd ever met." Trace welcomed the normal huskiness in his voice, a remnant of the embassy attack. Otherwise, Cat might have sensed the heartfelt tenderness in his tone.

Her eyes misted with tears. "I was the lucky one. Until the bombing."

He pulled his gaze from her face in time to spot a battered pickup barreling around a curve and crossing the center line toward them. "Look out!"

Cat swerved toward the right. The tires of the SUV clung precariously to the shoulder of the road. Trace glanced out the window and saw a sheer drop of hundreds of feet. A river wound like a silver thread on the ravine floor below.

The oncoming truck barreled by in a vortex of wind and dust, and Cat barely managed to jerk her vehicle onto the highway.

"That idiot!" Cat exploded. "What the hell is he doing up here?"

"Who?"

She glanced in the rearview mirror at Megan, who apparently had slept through the entire hair-raising incident, and shook her head.

"Just some guy from town," she said between clenched teeth in a quieter voice.

Recognizing that she didn't want to talk in front of her daughter, Trace changed the subject. "You okay? That was a close call."

She nodded. But her breath came in shallow gasps, and her knuckles on the steering wheel were blanched from the fierceness of her grip.

"Your reflexes are quick," he said with admiration. "Otherwise we'd be swimming in that river down there."

Obviously shaken, she kept her eyes on the road ahead and didn't comment.

The silence gave him time to contemplate his upcoming meeting with Gabriel. He loved the taciturn old rancher who had served as a surrogate father to him, the only one he'd ever known. With regret, he reminded himself that, as with Cat, he'd have to treat the man like a stranger.

Gabe's still waters ran deep, though, and Trace would have to take special care not to give himself away. The old man's sharp blue eyes didn't miss much, and he had an uncanny habit of reading between the lines of what was said—and what was left unspoken.

Cat rounded the last curve, and Trace braced himself for his first view of High Valley Ranch in over five years, with its rolling meadows and woodlands surrounded by towering snow-crested peaks.

Home.

Not exactly the homecoming he'd anticipated, however.

The gate to High Valley Ranch that usually stood

open wide in welcome was closed tight. An old man stood before the gate, hammering a large sign onto its cross posts.

No Trespassing.

At the car's approach, the man looked up. With a shock of surprise, Trace recognized the stoop-shouldered, white-haired figure by his blazing blue eyes.

"That's Daddy." Cat pulled the vehicle to a stop in front of the closed gate and slid from the car. Through the open door, Trace could hear their conversation.

"What are you doing?" she called to Gabe.

"You're a smart girl." Gabe kept his eyes on his hammering. "You figure it out."

"I know what the sign says, Dad. What I don't understand is why. We've never posted the ranch before."

"Snake Larson was here today."

Trace remembered the troublemaker vividly, recalled how he'd bothered Cat when she was younger and wondered how much of a nuisance Snake had been to the Ericksons while Trace had been in Tabari. His frustration at the loss of five years grew deeper. With Marc's death, Megan's birth and pond scum like Snake annoying her, Cat had needed him.

And he hadn't been here for her.

"I saw Snake," Cat told her father. "He almost ran us off the road. What did he want?"

"You." Gabe swung the hammer with ruthless fury and attacked a nail that attached a corner of the sign to the gate. "He was planning to settle down and wait until you came home from school. Said he wasn't afraid of my shooting him this time. Said he'd figured I was too decent and law-abiding to make that kind of mistake."

"Then why did he leave?"

"Told him it was true that I'm decent and law-abiding. That's why people would believe me when I said my gun went off accidentally and shattered his kneecap." Gabe gave the nail another vicious whack. "Snake fell all over himself getting out of here then."

Trace chuckled. Adversity may have taken its toll, but it hadn't broken Gabe's crusty spirit.

"If Snake's gone," Cat said, "why post the signs?"

"So if he comes back, I can have the sheriff arrest him for trespassing. Then maybe the big jerk will leave us alone."

Gabe finished driving another nail, then tossed the hammer through the open window of his truck, parked by the gate. For the first time, he glanced up and spotted Trace in the front seat of Cat's SUV.

"Who's that?"

"Company. I'll meet you at the house and introduce you."

After pecking a kiss on Gabe's leathered cheek, Cat swung gracefully into the driver's seat.

"Trouble?" Trace asked.

She shook her head. "Nothing Dad and I can't handle."

Gabe opened the gate and waved them through before heading to his truck.

Trace's attention was captured by the view on the three-mile drive from the gate to the ranchhouse. He and Marc had covered every inch of this land on foot and on horseback. To someone raised on the mean streets of Chicago, the ranch had seemed like paradise, and many times in Tabari, before he'd lost his memories, Trace had wondered whether he'd inflated the land's beauty and magnificence in his mind.

He hadn't.

If anything, the land was more majestic than he'd remembered. The crisp, clean mountain air filled his lungs with intoxicating freshness, and the deep hues of the grass, forests and sky were postcard perfect. The car approached the hillock where the two-story log ranch house sat overlooking the valley, and he felt he had truly come home at last. The long and low building's broad front porch ran the length of its facade, and pots of flaming red geraniums flanked the wide front steps, just as they had when he left five years ago.

Nothing had changed.

And everything had changed.

Cat stopped the car beside the front walk and glanced at him. "You okay?"

For a moment he couldn't speak. When he finally found his voice, it trembled with emotion. "I was thinking of Marc and Ryan. No wonder they loved this place so much. It looks like heaven on earth, just like they said."

Cat sighed. "It will never be the same without them, that's for sure."

She slipped from the car and circled it. Trace climbed from his seat and watched her open the rear door. Megan lay sound asleep in her carrier, her cheeks flushed, her tiny pink mouth drawn in a bewitching bow shape.

Cat picked her up without waking her and whispered to him, "I'll take her up to her room so she can nap until supper. She always plays herself out at the sitter's."

"Want me to carry her?" Trace hungered for the sensation of his daughter in his arms.

Cat shook her head. "She's not that heavy, and I won't be but a minute."

Trace followed Cat up the porch steps, opened the front door for her and followed her inside.

Cat nodded toward the right. "You can wait in there. Dad was right behind us. He'll be here soon."

Trace watched until Cat disappeared around the landing of the wide stairway in the central hall, then stepped into the great room he recalled so vividly. Again, nothing had changed. The same high, vaulted ceiling with its ponderosa pine beams arched above the spacious pine-paneled room. At the far end, a bank of floor-to-ceiling windows surrounded a fireplace made of river rock and flooded the entire area with brilliant late afternoon light.

Deep sofas covered with butter-soft leather in earth tones circled the fireplace, and bright Navajo and other Native American rugs covered the floor. The only new addition Trace could spot was a table in the corner near the fireplace topped with framed portraits of Marc and Ryan in dress uniform, flanked by vases of fresh flowers from Cat's perennial garden.

Like a shrine.

With Marc's death still fresh and hurting, Trace studied his buddy's picture. "I miss you, cowboy," he murmured. "You should be here. It's not right without you."

He swiveled at the sound of footsteps in the hall, clasped his hands behind him and surveyed the mountains through the tall windows.

"Megan never even stirred," Cat said behind him. "She must have been exhausted."

Trace turned to face her, and Gabriel entered the room.

"Now, Catherine," her father demanded, "who's this visitor you were telling me about?"

"Trace Gallagher." Trace extended his hand, exerting all his self-control not to encompass Gabe in a bear hug.

"He was a friend of Marc's and Ryan's," Cat explained.

Gabe didn't accept Trace's hand. Instead, he narrowed his sharp blue eyes and scrutinized Trace within an inch of his life.

"Marc never spoke of you," Gabe said in a voice heavy with suspicion. "Ryan, either."

"Trace was working undercover," Cat hastened to explain. "He has a letter of introduction from Colonel Barker at the embassy—"

"Letters can be forged," Gabe said with an impatient shake of his head without taking his gaze off Trace.

"Daddy!" Cat's famous blush glowed deep red in the room's bright sunlight.

Trying to appear nonchalant, Trace shrugged, but his brain was working a mile a minute. Gabe's instincts were never wrong, and although the old man hadn't recognized him, he'd picked up immediately that something wasn't quite right. Trace would need some fast talking and heavy backpedaling to win the old man over, convince him of the false identity.

The lives of the entire Erickson family depended on it.

"Why would I want to forge a letter, Mr. Erickson?" he asked with more calm than he felt.

"Why have you shown up here years after Marc and Ryan died without us ever having heard of you?" Gabe shot the question at him. "Your name wasn't among the letters of condolence."

"No, sir. For the first eighteen months after Ryan died, I was hospitalized, recovering from the injuries I sustained in the bombing."

Cat gasped. "You were there?"

Trace nodded. "Guarding the prince."

"Then you saw Ryan when the embassy—" She shook her head and held up her hands. "No, don't tell me. It's better I don't know."

"He died instantly," Trace lied, his voice soft, consoling. "He didn't suffer."

Her face pale, Cat sank into the nearest chair. "You saw him…die?"

"Yes." He hated the pain he was causing her, despised his deception, but he loved her too much to risk the truth.

Tears flooded her eyes. "I'd always hoped…"

"Hoped what?" he asked gently.

She lifted her head and looked straight at him. "They never found his body. I've always hoped there was some mistake, that someday Ryan would come home."

"I'm sorry," Trace said earnestly, sorry for more than she could know.

"So why *are* you here?" Gabe insisted.

"Your daughter invited me. But if you have a problem with that, I can head back to town."

"You have no transportation, and it's forty miles," Cat objected.

Trace faced Gabriel. "Forty miles is no obstacle to a Marine."

The faintest hint of a smile played across Gabe's rugged features. "To a Marine in new boots that aren't broken in yet, it could be a hell of a trek. Sit down, son. I'll pour us a drink."

Trace sat, but he knew Gabe well enough to realize the old man's suspicions had yet to be laid to rest.

Chapter Five

While Gabriel filled glasses with bourbon and spring water at the sideboard, Cat studied Trace. No wonder her father's suspicious nature had kicked into high gear at the stranger's arrival.

Trace Gallagher was an enigma.

He'd appeared out of nowhere, claiming to know Ryan and Marc. She had accepted his letter of introduction at face value, not even considering, as Gabe had instantly, that such papers could be fabricated. Her unsatisfied craving for more information about Ryan's final days had overwhelmed her caution.

Too bad that intense yearning for news hadn't overwhelmed her other senses, as well.

They, unfortunately, had kicked into overdrive at Trace's arrival and had yet to settle down. Her eyes feasted on the sight of his long, lean body, stretched out in Ryan's favorite chair beside the fireplace, the striking planes and angles of his handsome face, the grace of his long, slender hands, their appeal unmarred by several angry scars that disappeared beneath the cuffs of his chambray shirt.

Her ears savored the seductive music of his voice that, in its low huskiness, sounded as if he'd just awakened from a deep sleep each time he spoke. Even above the fragrance of the flowers in the room and the scent of dead ashes in the hearth, her nose could detect his haunting and uniquely masculine scent. Her hands itched to—

With a sudden mental shock, she cut short her musings. The man was a puzzle, a stranger, possibly a dangerous stranger. She had no business indulging in flights of imagination over someone she knew nothing about. He'd spend the night, and tomorrow he'd be gone.

And that prospect brought her no happiness. She had to be crazy for wanting to know him better, but that was exactly what she wanted.

Gabe handed Trace a drink. "So, Mr. Gallagher, why *are* you here?"

"It's Lieutenant Gallagher, but you're welcome to call me Trace." Trace accepted the glass with a nod of thanks. "I'm on leave."

"But why here?" Gabe persisted and sagged into the chair opposite Trace.

Cat gazed at her father with concern. He'd always been slow to warm up to people. He hadn't really accepted Ryan until the second time he visited the ranch with Marc. But since their deaths, her dad had become even more skeptical, cynical and crotchety. He took nothing—and no one—at face value.

Especially strangers.

Trace lifted his glass toward Marc and Ryan's photographs. "To absent friends."

Tears clouded Cat's eyes at the gesture.

"Amen to that." Gabe joined the toast, then tossed back a deep swallow. "But you still haven't answered my question. Why have you come here?"

"Marc and Ryan told him about Montana," Cat explained in an attempt to rationalize her hasty and probably not-too-smart invitation, "and our ranch in particular. He wanted to see it for himself."

His gaze still suspicious, her father peered at Trace over the rim of his glass. "Marc and Ryan had been stationed in Tabari only a matter of weeks before the bombing. If you were busy working for Prince Asim, you didn't have time to get to know them well."

"We were friends before we reached Tabari," Trace said. "We went through basic training together at Parris Island, and later at Camp LeJeune and Officers' Candidate School."

"So you say." Her father obviously wasn't accepting any of Trace's claims.

Cat expected Trace to bristle at her father's disbelief. Instead, he turned to her with a slow, easy smile that jolted her like an electric shock. "Ryan gave me a sample of the fudge you sent him that first week, the one made with macadamia nuts. Best candy I ever tasted."

Cat noticed her father grow still, impressed by Trace's knowledge. Gabe's eyes had lost their skeptical cast and were assessing their visitor with new interest.

"And halfway through basic—" Trace shifted his attention to her father "—Marc was frantic to come home to help fight the forest fires that were threatening your tract of timber near the Canadian border, but he wasn't able to swing a leave."

Cat shuddered, remembering how close the flames had come to High Valley, how only the diligence of the Forest Service crews and a lucky downpour had saved the ranch.

"And I remember Ryan's heel blisters that refused to heal," Trace said, "the ones he developed on a forced march through the South Carolina swamp."

"So," Gabe said with a bittersweet smile, "looks like you really did know my boys."

"Yes, sir. I considered Marc—" Trace's voice broke on her brother's name "—and Ryan my best friends."

"What else do you remember from their Parris Island days?" Gabriel leaned forward, his hands clenched around his glass, his eyes shining.

Cat gave herself a shake. "While you two take a trip down memory lane, I have supper to cook."

She left them chatting happily and headed toward the kitchen. After seeing her father's interest perk up at Trace's recollections, she decided that bringing the stranger home for a visit hadn't been such a bad idea, after all. Gabe hadn't seemed so engrossed in anything in a long time.

Now all she had to do was keep her unwanted reactions to the handsome Marine under control until he packed up and left. The last thing she needed was involvement with another military intelligence operative who would head off to risk life and limb on the other side of the world.

DERRICK HUTTON sat in the shadows, waiting for a knock on his door. A man of average height and average weight with nondescript features that wouldn't stand out in a crowd, he possessed the perfect appearance for his line of work. He could easily slip in and out of a room without calling attention to himself, walk down a street unnoticed, defy description even by a trained observer.

Tonight, however, his skills at anonymity were of no use. What he needed was information. His mind still wrestled with the puzzle of Trace Gallagher, his thoughts returning again and again to the former bodyguard like a tongue seeks out a sore tooth. In Hutton's three-year tenure as a civilian employee of the American embassy in Tabari's capital of Bahira, he had never seen or heard of the man, and Hutton had made a point of knowing *everyone* in both the embassy and the prince's palace.

Odd that only after the bombing had Gallagher surfaced as one of Prince Asim's bodyguards. Had he been hired just prior to the bombing?

That's what Hutton wanted to believe, but his gut told him that Gallagher was trouble with a capital T. The terrorist didn't dare make a move against Gallagher until he had more facts. Calling attention to their group by going after a nobody was the last complication he wanted.

A sudden rapping at the door interrupted his thoughts. With swift, silent steps, he crossed the room and leaned close to the door.

"Who is it?"

The answer came, a password spoken softly in perfect Arabic. Hutton opened the door only wide enough for his visitor to slide through before closing and locking it. He motioned the newcomer to a chair, then crossed to the television set, clicked it on and turned up the volume. If for any reason he was under surveillance, the canned laughter of the sitcom would drown their conversation.

Hutton sat across from his visitor, and the man leaned forward, his mouth close to Hutton's ear.

"We could learn nothing of Gallagher's interrogation at the Pentagon. Our informant is good, but his security clearance level is not high enough to access those files."

Hutton sighed in disgust. "Couldn't your contact just hack into the computer and find what he needed?"

"If he wanted to call attention to himself—and to us."

The man had a point. "What *did* he discover?"

"Where Gallagher went when he left the Pentagon." His visitor's eyes gleamed with triumph.

Hutton waited a moment. "Are you going to tell me, or must I beat it out of you?"

"A military transport conveyed him to Great Falls, Montana. From there he took a bus to Athens in the northwest corner of the state."

"His home?"

The visitor shook his head. "According to our research, Gallagher is from Syracuse."

"Then what is he doing in Montana?" Hutton demanded. "Fly-fishing?"

"He was seen later that day in the company of Catherine Erickson, a local high school teacher."

"Erickson?" The pieces fell together. "Any relation to Marc Erickson?"

"His sister."

"Why would he visit Erickson's sister?"

"She's more than that," the visitor said. "Catherine Erickson was engaged to Ryan Christopher."

Alarms sounded in Hutton's brain. "Why would the Pentagon send Gallagher to the Ericksons? If Erickson or Christopher had told the family anything more about the embassy bombing, wouldn't they have passed it on to the authorities by now?"

"Gallagher could have finished his business at the Pentagon," the visitor said. "His trip to Montana could be just a social call to the family of old friends."

Hutton searched his memories. He'd never laid eyes on Gallagher before the bombing. After the bombing, Christopher was dead and Erickson in a coma. How could Gallagher have known either of the two Marine lieutenants who had almost foiled Hutton's perfect plan? If Hutton hadn't managed to catch up with Erickson in the alley near the embassy, the man would have lived to implicate him. As it was, his shot to Erickson's back had been a lucky one.

Although the Marine had told his pals who found him that Ryan knew the identity of the man who'd shot him, Erickson had lost consciousness without implicating Hutton. Christopher was dead, and Erickson had finally died without ever emerging from his coma.

So where the hell did Gallagher fit in?

"I'll take care of this," Hutton said, rising to indicate the meeting was ended.

As soon as his visitor had left, he picked up the telephone. He had an operative in Spokane, just a few hours away from the small Montana town. Before he could move forward with plans for the next bombing, Hutton had to know that Gallagher wasn't a threat.

THE NEXT MORNING, Cat hummed contentedly under her breath while she made coffee. Morning was always her favorite time of day, and today was especially pleasant, filled with memories of last night's lively dinner. For over two hours, Trace in his distinctive husky voice had entertained them with stories of Marc and Ryan's adventures as Marine recruits in the Carolinas and interpreters in Tabari. For that short time, Marc and Ryan had seemed alive again.

Something else had stirred to life in Cat yesterday, as well, but she couldn't quite put her finger on it. She acknowledged her attraction to Trace, but whether her interest was sparked by his stories of Ryan, the resemblance of his physical build and amazing eyes to her fiancé, or the unique qualities of Trace himself, she couldn't be sure. Wishing she could understand the contentment she experienced in his presence and why she felt such an incredible pull toward the stranger, she hurried to peel potatoes for hash browns before Megan awoke.

Pale early morning light streamed through the tall east windows with their jaunty yellow-blue-and-white plaid curtains. With its cheerful yellow walls, mellow pine cabinets and her mother's collection of Blue Willow platters lining the plate rails, the sunny kitchen always lifted her spirits. But the main reason the room was her favorite was the memories it held of the hours she'd shared there with Ryan, who'd always helped with the dishes.

Trace had surprised her last night by insisting on clearing the table and offering to do dishes, but she'd shooed him away to join her father in front of the fire. She'd been motivated partly by how much her father had enjoyed Trace's anecdotes at supper but also by a reluctance to share the intimacy of her kitchen with him.

She lifted her head at the sound of footsteps at the back door. After wiping their boots on the outside mat, Gabe and Trace entered the room together. Trace had offered to assist Gabe with the horses that morning, and her father, happy to show off his prize stock, had led him to the barn.

For a greenhorn New Englander, Cat thought, except for the newness of his clothes, Trace looked as if he'd worked a ranch his entire life.

"Coffee smells great," Trace said with a smile that led her thoughts in dangerous directions.

"Help yourself to a cup," Gabe instructed. "Mugs are in the cabinet by the sink."

Cat pulled her attention from their handsome visitor and focused a worried gaze on her father. This morning his usually clear blue eyes appeared rheumy, his suntanned nose glowed red, and as she watched he erupted in an explosive sneeze that he barely managed to muffle in a red bandanna jerked hastily from his back pocket.

"You're not catching cold?" she asked.

Wiping his nose, he shook his head.

"Been taking your allergy medicine?"

Looking sheepish, her father admitted, "This hay fever's my own danged fault. You know I don't like swallowing pills."

Trace handed him a steaming mug of coffee. "Maybe this will help."

"Thanks." Gabe settled at the kitchen table and wrapped his fingers around the warm mug.

Trace brought his own mug and sat across from Cat.

"Cream and sugar?" she asked Trace, knowing her father always drank his coffee black.

"Sugar, please."

She rose, removed the sugar bowl from the cabinet and passed it to their visitor. Trace heaped three teaspoons into his cup and swirled the spoon in a gesture that brought back a flood of memories.

"That's the way Ryan always drank his coffee," Cat said.

As if caught by surprise, Trace wavered briefly,

then returned to his stirring. "Never used sugar until I started working for the prince. His household likes their coffee sweet. They drink it almost like syrup."

After another mighty sneeze, Gabe pushed to his feet. "Looks like I'll have to take those blasted pills, after all. Sorry, Gallagher, but I won't be able to show you the ranch on horseback today. The danged medication always puts me to sleep when I first start taking it."

"Sorry you're not feeling well," Trace commiserated. "Maybe Cat could show me around. You ride, don't you, Cat?"

Gabe chuckled. "Cat ride? She was on a horse before she learned to walk."

"But I can't leave Megan, and the trek around the ranch is too long for her. If she goes with us, she'll be exhausted."

She felt torn between wanting to spend the morning with Trace and reluctance to expose herself further to his charm. Although last night her father had invited him to stay for a few days, Trace would still be leaving soon, never to return. She saw no point in forming an attachment, and Trace, as Ryan had been, was the kind of man she could learn to like too much too fast.

"I'll watch Megan," Gabe said.

"You can't watch her if you're asleep," Cat protested, thinking that settled the issue.

"If I can borrow a horse, I can mosey about by myself," Trace offered.

"Nonsense," Gabe said. "You won't know where to go. Cat can show you the high spots of our spread.

I'll call Myra MacIntosh—she's our nearest neighbor—and ask her to stay with Megan this morning."

Not wanting to appear inhospitable, Cat smiled at Trace. "We'll start out after breakfast."

His long, collected look from those khaki-brown eyes made her catch her breath. "I'm looking forward to it."

AFTER BREAKFAST, Cat told Megan where she and Trace were going.

"I wanna go wif you," her daughter insisted, fists on her hips, chin jutting. "I like Trace."

"Can you ride a horse?" Obvious amusement tugged at the corners of Trace's mouth.

Megan shook her head. "Not a horse. A pony."

As if mesmerized by the little girl, Trace stooped to her eye level. "Do you have your own pony?"

Megan nodded. "Her name's Sugar."

Sugar, Cat remembered with a pang of regret, was Ryan's public term of endearment. In private, he called her *Kalila.*

"Sugar. I like that name," Trace said. "How did you pick it?"

"That's what my daddy used to call my mommy. Mommy told me. She tells me lots of stories about Daddy and Uncle Marc."

Something glittered in Trace's eyes, and for a moment Cat thought she'd seen tears, but he blinked, and the impression passed. It must have been a trick of the light.

"Can I come, Mommy? Please."

Cat found it difficult to deny her daughter anything, but she'd learned not to spoil her completely. "Sorry, sweetheart, but we'll be gone too long and you'd get too tired."

Megan's lower lip trembled, and Cat relented. "But if you're a good girl for Grandpa and Mrs. Mac, I'll take you for a ride after lunch, okay?"

Her daughter looked at Trace. "Will you come, too?"

"If your mother wants me to."

At that moment, Mrs. MacIntosh, the plump and pretty elderly neighbor who operated the adjoining dairy farm with her husband, arrived. With sparkling brown eyes, a sunny disposition, the energy of a woman half her age and a dozen grandchildren, Mrs. Mac considered Megan one of her granddaughters. The little girl adored her.

Cat introduced Mrs. Mac to Trace, explained about Gabe's allergies and gave her instructions for Megan.

"Come along, dearie," Mrs. Mac told Megan. "You're still in your jammies. Let's get you bathed and dressed."

"Thanks for helping out," Cat said. "Dad's lying down in his room."

The friendly woman shook her head and clicked her tongue in disapproval. "Men. They never do what the doctor tells them. Afraid it'll ruin their manly image. If Gabe weren't so miserable, I'd say it serves him right, but he's suffered too much the last few years. His allergies only add insult to injury."

"Come here, sweetie," Cat said to Megan, "and give me a kiss before I go."

She leaned down, and Megan threw her arms around her mother's neck and planted a loud smack on her lips. Cat straightened, and Megan turned to Trace. "Want one, too?"

Trace's expression transformed at the question, his face reflecting such hunger and tenderness, it was almost painful to behold. Cat could almost understand. He looked the way she felt whenever she watched her daughter, but Cat was Megan's mother. For her, such a reaction was natural, expected. Trace's was a total surprise and inexplicable. Did the man long so much for children of his own?

Before Cat could sort out her thoughts, Trace's hungry look dissolved into a warm smile. "Sure, I'd like a kiss, but only if it's all right with your mother. You should never, ever kiss strangers."

Megan glanced at Cat, and she nodded her approval.

Kneeling to face Megan, Trace opened his arms. Megan flew into them, hugged his neck and noisily kissed his cheek. Then she drew back, gazed at him with serious hazel eyes and patted his tanned cheek with her tiny fingers. "Hold on tight and don't go too fast."

Trace glanced at Cat and cocked an eyebrow in question.

"That's what I tell her when she rides Sugar," Cat explained.

"You're right," Trace said solemnly to the little girl. "I'll be very careful."

"You don't want to fall off and break your neck," Megan said with a superior nod.

Trace looked at Cat, who was trying not to laugh. "You tell her that, too?"

Cat grinned. "That piece of sterling advice comes from her grandfather. You're stalling, young lady. Run upstairs for your bath."

"Yes, ma'am." With Mrs. Mac at her heels, Megan scampered up the stairs.

"She's adorable." Trace rose to his full height, watched Megan until she disappeared around the landing, then faced Cat. "You've done a great job with her. Being a single parent can't be easy."

"Dad helps. You like children, don't you?"

Trace nodded, his expression wistful. "I've always wanted children of my own."

"Then you should have them." The encouragement popped out before Cat had time to consider that his reasons for not having a family were personal. Trace, however, didn't appear to take offense at her suggestion.

"Have to find me a wife first," he said easily.

"A good-looking man like you, that shouldn't be a problem," Cat said.

"You volunteering?"

The sudden impulse to say yes blindsided her, and she compensated with a deep, steadying breath. "Having lived around military men for so many years, I've been drilled thoroughly into never volunteering for anything.''

"Smart lady.''

She exhaled a sigh of relief, glad the dizzying moment had passed.

He followed her out the back door, and together they strolled across the yard toward the barn.

"Chickens—'' he pointed to the outbuildings "—and a vegetable garden. Looks like you're pretty self-sufficient here.''

Cat nodded, glad the conversation had turned less personal. "With milk and butter from the MacIntosh dairy, even if the roads become impassable in winter, we eat well.''

"Must take a lot of work.''

"We manage.''

She kept to herself her concern that the load was becoming more than she and her father could bear alone. Her thoughts turned to Todd Brewster. In his marriage proposals, he'd offered to help Gabe with the ranch, if that was where Cat would rather live. He'd promised he would have time to work the ranch before and after school and in the summers, and his offer had been tempting. His help might mean the difference between keeping the place going or selling out and moving into town.

The only problem was, fond as she was of Todd, she didn't love him the way she'd loved Ryan. She doubted she'd ever love any man that way again. She breathed a heavy sigh and could almost feel her shoulders bending beneath the weight of her problems. She had more than her own feelings to consider, she reminded herself sternly. Megan came first—and her daughter needed a father. Todd would make an ideal stepfather.

And there was her father to consider, too. He had already lost so much. It would kill him to lose his ranch, too.

Shaking off her musings, she caught Trace studying her curiously from the corner of his eye. She knew he'd registered her sigh, but he was almost a total stranger, and she wasn't about to burden him with her dilemma.

They entered the barn, and her eyes adjusted from the bright morning light to the dim interior. From the stall at the far end, Snickers, her dappled gray mare, bobbed her head in welcome. They strode through the center aisle, and Trace stopped at the stall on the right and approached Rogue, Ryan's chestnut quarter horse. Before Cat could warn him that the horse didn't like people, he was stroking Rogue's muzzle, and Rogue was gently nuzzling Trace's shoulder in return.

"He's a beauty," Trace said. "What's his name?"

Cat had to swallow her amazement to answer. "Rogue. He was Ryan's horse. You must be really good with animals. Rogue never allows anyone but Dad or me near him."

Trace reached higher and scratched behind Rogue's ears. "Seems gentle enough. May I ride him?"

The horse whinnied softly as if in approval.

"He's thrown everyone who's tried since Ryan..."

Died.

Even after five years, she had a hard time saying the word.

"But you still keep him?" Trace asked in a voice that seemed oddly filled with emotion.

"Ryan would have wanted me to."

Selling Rogue would have produced enough funds to hire temporary help, but even that would be only a stopgap measure in the long run. Having the horse was like having a little bit of Ryan left, and she didn't want to let go. Her father understood. They still kept Marc's horse, too.

Trace had stopped stroking the horse at her declaration, but he didn't turn. Rogue arched forward and nuzzled Trace's shoulder again.

"See," he said, "he likes me."

Still astonished at Rogue's reaction, Cat shrugged. "It's your neck, if you want to risk it. Saddles and bridles are over here."

A few minutes later, they were mounted and headed up the gravel road toward the north pasture. The morning, although sunny, was comfortably cool, and the air was laden with the fragrance of wildflowers and the resinous scent of evergreens. Sunlight glistened off the snow-covered peaks that surrounded the high alpine valley like the sides of a bowl, and the trill of birdsong and the occasional darting shadows of wings floated across the meadow.

In spite of the problems that weighed on her mind, Cat was surprised to find her mood as bright and sunny as the morning sky. She couldn't remember feeling this lighthearted since before Ryan's death and wondered whether it was the memories of Ryan that Trace had shared or the fascinating man himself who'd unburdened her heart.

Trace stopped, stood tall in the saddle and took a deep breath. "I've never smelled air so clean."

"Not even in the desert?" Cat asked.

He made a sour face and shook his head. "In Tabari we usually had the stench from the oil fields and refineries. Or so much sand blowing that we were afraid to breathe too deeply. Here, it's like inhaling a crisp vintage wine. Pretty heady stuff."

His boyish enthusiasm was infectious, and Cat found herself appreciating anew the clean and crisp atmosphere she usually took for granted.

"And the view," he said, "it's incredible. No wonder Marc and Ryan wanted to give up the military for this."

She nudged Snickers with her heels, and Trace and Rogue followed them off the road into the pasture, wading easily through the thick, high grass.

"Are you a career man?" she asked. "In for the long haul?"

His expression sobered. "Probably. Don't know what else I'd do."

"You could teach."

He shot her a surprised glance. "Teach what?"

"After living in the palace, aren't you fluent in Arabic? I'm sure not many have your language qualifications. You shouldn't have any trouble finding a job."

"I don't have the patience to teach. All those students would drive me nuts."

"You might be surprised."

"Do you like teaching?" he asked, so skillfully shifting the conversation that she didn't notice until later that he'd avoided talking about himself.

"I love it! But—" She stopped, embarrassed and reluctant to discuss her worries on such a gorgeous morning with a man she hardly knew.

"But what?" he prodded.

His eyes held such genuine interest, such gentle kindness, she couldn't help confiding in him. "But I'd rather spend more time with Megan."

"Why don't you?"

"Can't afford it."

"Didn't you get Marc's military benefits or life insurance? If they were anything like mine, they should have left you with enough to take a few years off from teaching, at least until Megan goes to school."

"Round-the-clock nursing care for Marc used most of the money—that, and hiring temporary help for Dad. We're barely making ends meet now *with* my teaching salary."

She halted, amazed that she had blurted out such intimate details. He must think her an idiot. But when she looked at Trace, his expression was compassionate, understanding.

"It's been hard for you, hasn't it?" he asked gently.

At the empathy in his voice, she fought back tears.

"At least I'm alive. And I have Megan. Marc and Ryan…"

Struggling for composure, she urged Snickers down the riverbank and into the icy water. About a foot deep, the swiftly moving current swirled around the horse's legs. "We'll cross here."

"Where are we going?"

She pointed to a rise on the other side of the river. "We couldn't have crossed last week except at the bridge south of here. With the snowmelt, the river was running six feet deep even here at the ford."

Trace angled Rogue into the shallow water, and she marveled again at his expert handling of the cantankerous horse no one but Ryan had been able to control.

On the other side of the river, they climbed a high hill. Before they reached the summit, Cat stopped and turned in the saddle to gaze behind her.

"You can see the whole ranch from here," she explained with a wave of her arm that took in the entire spread. "It's the best viewpoint on the property."

The ranch house, barn, corral and outbuildings perched in the distance like a miniature village, surrounded by rolling pastures flecked with dark spots of color from the sleek hides of the herd, glistening in the sunlight among the lush grass. Dark, primeval forests edged the spacious bowl of meadowland and climbed the steep slopes of the surrounding mountains until the tree line gave way to barren stretches of rocks and snow.

As always, a gamut of emotions flooded her as she contemplated High Valley. Pride, contentment and affection she was accustomed to, but recently a new feeling had been added to the mix, a nagging fear she might have to give up the home that had been in her family for five generations.

She glanced at Trace and was astonished at the look of longing on his expressive face, evident even beneath the shadow of his wide-brimmed Stetson, a yearning so intense it made her ache to witness it. His parents were dead, he'd told her. Maybe what she'd noted in his wistful expression was his desire for a home of his own.

"Come on," she said. "There's a special place I want to show you."

They crested the hill, and she was pleased to note that the tall grass had been neatly trimmed inside the picket fence that encircled the hilltop. For generations, the small cemetery had served as a resting place for the Erickson family.

She slid from her saddle and tied Snickers's reins to a fence post. Trace did the same for Rogue and followed her through the well-oiled gate.

"We brought Marc and Ryan home," she said, pointing to the granite gravestones marked with the Marine insignia and their names, birth and death dates. Colorful flowers bloomed at the base of the markers, and recently planted shrubs of rosemary for remembrance. "Marc was laid to rest beside our mother."

With a stunned look on his face, Trace removed

his hat, approached the graves and knelt beside Marc's stone. Without a word, he laid his hand on the smooth granite and closed his eyes. His sense of loss reverberated through Cat, and if she hadn't known before, she was absolutely convinced at that moment how much he'd loved her brother.

She longed to go to Trace, to put her arms around him and comfort him. To be comforted and share their mutual loss. Even more, to feel the heat of him beneath her hands, the thunder of his heart beneath her cheek, to yield her mouth, her body, her heart to him...

Dazed and disturbed by her unexpected and inexplicable desire, she moved toward the gate, leaving Trace alone with his grief, giving herself space to analyze her puzzling and irrational response to a man she scarcely knew. For years, she'd believed she could never love a man, never yearn for him, never react to his touch as she had to Ryan.

Her response to Trace Gallagher had blown her assumptions into smithereens. The knowledge left her giddy and shaking, and she thrust her hands into the pockets of her jeans to hide their trembling. Maybe too many years of sexual abstinence had unbalanced her hormones.

And her brain.

After several minutes, Trace stood and cleared his throat, then gazed at Ryan's headstone with a puzzled frown. "You brought Ryan home?"

Cat braced herself for the pain that had always felt

as fresh and sharp as it had five years ago, but today it had miraculously eased in Trace's presence.

"We buried his dogtags, some pictures, a few of his favorite books...that's all there was."

Trace turned away, as if to be alone with his grief. He walked to the edge of the plot and lifted his head toward the surrounding mountains.

Suddenly, his shoulders stiffened and his muscles tensed.

"Look." He pointed to a spot just below the saddleback of Preacher's Ridge. "Do you see that?"

Cat followed his arm and noted two spots of sunlight flashing off glass. "The reflection? I see it."

"What's up there?" Trace asked.

"Nothing. It's a wilderness area set aside by the Forest Service."

"Any trails?"

"No." Cat shivered at the gravity in his voice and shook her head. "Why?"

"Because that light's reflecting off binocular lenses. Someone's watching your ranch."

Chapter Six

"It's probably just some hiker taking in the scenery," Cat assured Trance.

"Those lenses haven't moved," Trace protested, keeping his tone purposely calm while wondering if he was overreacting. "Whoever it is, he's studying the ranch. See? He hasn't shifted focus the whole time we've been watching."

"Like I said, maybe it's a tourist who likes the view. A greenhorn like you," she teased, "who's never seen a ranch before."

Cat tossed her head, sending her golden blond hair flying around her attractive face and seemingly unconcerned by his worry.

"Besides," she insisted, "why would anyone case our ranch? We have nothing of value except cattle, and unless rustlers put wings on the herd or move them up over the mountains through dense forests and impossibly steep terrain, the only way to drive them out of here is the road we came in on. Any cow thieves would be caught and arrested before they got as far as the MacIntosh farm."

Trace kept his eyes on the stationary twin reflections on the ridge above. His experience with terrorists had made him paranoid, or at the very least ultrasuspicious.

His notice of the watcher on the ridge, however, had stopped him just in time from making a terrible mistake. Moved by the sight of Marc's grave—and his own, so carefully tended—and the obvious devotion of the woman he loved to her lost fiancé, he'd almost blurted out the truth to Cat. Overcome with emotion, he'd been on the verge of taking her in his arms and revealing his identity. Only the sight of the binocular reflections on the ridge had saved him, reminding him of the possible danger she faced.

"Maybe it's that Snake what's his name," Trace suggested. "The man who almost ran us off the road yesterday."

"Snake?" Her voice rose with skepticism. "It's a long, steep climb through thick underbrush to the top of that ridge. Snake's too lazy and out of shape for such a trek. If Snake Larson's going to cause trouble, believe me, it'll be the in-your-face kind."

Pulling his attention from the ridge, he turned to find Cat watching him, a furrow of worry between her brows replacing her formerly untroubled smile, and he silently cursed himself for bothering her with what was probably nothing of concern, only a curious hiker like she'd said. She had enough troubles without his adding more.

He gave himself a mental shake. Cat was right. Snake wouldn't have made the effort to climb the ridge. And Trace was probably being paranoid about terrorists. As long as they had no idea who Trace was, they had no reason to follow him or keep the Erickson ranch under surveillance. His deliberations reminded him of his mission. Gabe and Cat had invited him to spend a few days with them. That didn't give him much time to find out whether Marc had communicated anything that might lead to the terrorists.

The Pentagon shrinks had hoped returning to the ranch and seeing Cat would jog his memories. She'd shaken loose memories, all right, remembrances that made being unable to touch her an almost unbearable torture. So far, however, those ten crucial days prior to the embassy bombing remained as much a blank as ever.

For now, his only hope for clues to the terrorists' identities would have to come from something Marc might have said to his family. But questions about Marc's illness would be painful for Cat and Gabe, and Trace wasn't looking forward to probing those emotional wounds.

Purposely turning his back on the watcher on the ridge, Trace draped his arm casually around Cat's shoulder, resisting the urge to pull her closer. She smelled of soap and sunshine with her signature hint of honeysuckle, and her scent brought back a hundred memories and roused his hunger for her. Keeping a tight rein on his feelings, he led her out of the tiny cemetery, carefully closed the gate behind them and released her with reluctance.

He turned his attention to Rogue. Pleased by how

well his horse remembered him, he swung into the saddle, and Cat mounted Snickers.

"What's next on the tour?" he asked.

"We'll cut through the forest, and I'll show you Daddy's timber."

Cat guided Snickers down the hill then up another slope toward the tree line, and with a last glance toward the ridge Trace edged Rogue beside her. She was probably right about the watcher being a hiker. He was glad she had shaken off her sorrow, that her frown had disappeared and that she once again seemed to be enjoying their ride.

"How long's it been since you had a day off?" he asked.

"A day off?" she said with a rueful smile. "What's that?"

"Time for yourself. Between your job, the ranch and taking care of your dad and Megan, you'll burn out fast without some time for relaxing."

"Relaxation is a luxury I can't afford."

"Suppose you had the time. What would you do?"

"Do?"

"For fun?"

She gave a self-deprecating snort. "What's fun?"

"When you were dating Ryan, there must have been things you enjoyed doing."

The blush that he loved started at the V in her blouse and worked its way up her face, enveloping her skin in a delightful rosy glow.

"Besides that," he teased.

She halted her horse just inside the tree line in the

shade of an immense Douglas fir and gazed over the meadow they'd crossed, but her eyes seemed glazed, as if she were looking inward. "Mostly we made plans for the future."

Today he could remember every cherished detail of those plans they'd made together, but just a few weeks ago, he'd been ignorant of everything.

Even though the amnesia hadn't been his fault, he felt inundated by guilt. While he had been blissfully unaware, living in comfort in Asim's palace, Cat, with her hopes and dreams smashed, had been struggling to keep the ranch going and to raise their daughter. Somehow he had to make up for all she'd endured alone over those long years. Some time for herself would be a small but symbolic start.

"If I could give you a whole day," he said, "to spend however you like, what would you do? Go shopping?"

He knew the answer, but he wanted to hear her say it. If he lived to be a hundred, he'd never tire of the lilting intonation of her voice.

Cat shook her head. "I must have been standing behind the door when they passed out that particular female gene. I've never liked to shop."

She edged Snickers into the trees along the shady trail that was just barely wide enough for Rogue to trot alongside her.

"How about a manicure?" he suggested. "And a massage?"

"Like at some fancy spa?" She grimaced with apparent distaste. "Waste of good money, as far as I'm concerned. I get the same results with an emery board and a good soak in the bathtub.''

His beloved Cat was as practical as ever. Getting her to pamper herself would take some doing.

"There must be something," he insisted in exasperation. It had been far too long since she'd taken time for herself if she couldn't even remember what she liked best.

"A good book is something I'd enjoy," she finally admitted. "And time to read it all the way through."

"What do you like to read?"

"Everything—mystery, romance, science fiction. Just so long as the story's good and the ending's happy."

She deserved happy endings. If he could help Wentworth nab the terrorists, she'd have one.

If not...

He hadn't considered the possibility of failure, even though his chances of success were slim. If he didn't find out or remember what he needed to know, he'd have to spend the rest of his life as Trace Gallagher. Failure meant losing Cat all over again. Only this time, he'd be losing his daughter, too. He shoved the disheartening possibility from his mind.

"Maybe I can give your dad a hand while I'm here. Then you can take that day off and enjoy a good book."

She eyed him sharply. "Why would you want to do that?"

Because I love you. Because it hurts to see you

working so hard, raising our child alone. Because you deserve to be looked after, cherished.

"Chalk it up to my Boy Scout background," he said easily, "and call it my good deed for the week."

"It wouldn't speak well of our Western hospitality if I let our guest work while I put my feet up."

Her words hardly registered. At the sight of a small glade off to the right, he'd halted Rogue and sat staring at the spot where Megan had been conceived. Dappled sunlight filtered through the majestic evergreens, filling the circular clearing with soft, golden light. Thick ferns carpeted the floor, and the unearthly quiet reminded him of a cathedral.

Cat stopped Snickers beside him. "You're not seeing rustlers again?"

In the shimmering light, she seemed as insubstantial as a dream but even more beautiful than the Cat he'd made love to in this very place so long ago. The gentle breeze lifted her hair from the slender column of her neck, her delicate eyebrows quirked in bewilderment, and those perceptive blue eyes met his with an intensity that pierced straight to the center of his being. More than anything, he wanted to dismount, pull her down beside him and love her with a fierceness that would erase the loneliness of those lost, wasted years.

He fought to bring his emotions in line and finally managed to speak in a normal voice. "Just admiring what a beautiful place this is."

Her questioning expression gave way to a look of tender contemplation. "Yes, it's very special."

As if unwilling to share the site with him, she dug her knees into Snickers's sides and moved ahead on the trail. With a last glance at what had been their favorite meeting place, he followed and caught up with her.

Soon the trail angled southward, then southeast, until they had doubled back to the river. Unlike the shallow, peaceful ford they had crossed earlier, the water at this point ran wide, deep and turbulent, frothing and foaming, and dropped rapidly in elevation over a series of jutting boulders and terraces carved out of the rock.

"This must be where Ryan and Marc went whitewater rafting," Trace shouted over the roar of the waterfalls.

Cat nodded, her hair glistening with drops of water like diamonds from the spray of the current. "There's another ford farther downstream. We can cross to the house there."

Along the river, the trail narrowed until they were forced to ride single file. Trace swung in behind Cat, and as he did, he caught a flash of color darting swiftly through the trees on the slope above them. He stopped and scoured the forest, searching for another sign of who or what was moving parallel to them above the trail. The rush of the water, surging over boulders, covered all other sounds.

Cat turned in the saddle and saw him stopped on the trail. "What is it?"

"Nothing."

He shook his head and urged Rogue forward. The

binoculars on the ridge had made him edgy. These forests teemed with wildlife. The movement he'd seen in the trees could have been a low-flying bird, a whitetail deer, even a brown bear. He had no reason to believe someone was watching them.

Except the strong feeling in his gut that, until now at least, had never been wrong.

TRACE GALLAGHER had turned strangely quiet on their ride home, and Cat wondered about the cause of his silence. She suspected their visit to the cemetery had made him introspective. His grief for his fallen friends had seemed strangely raw and fresh, untempered by time.

Of course, it could be he was quiet because he was all talked out after sharing so many stories of his life with Ryan and Marc.

Or perhaps, for some strange reason, the sight of someone watching the ranch had spooked him. While he'd contemplated the binoculars flashing on the ridge, his demeanor had grown still and deadly, reminding her of the lethal traps hunters set for bear—strong, silent and waiting to spring.

She discarded that last ridiculous notion, unable to think of a single reason someone's presence on the ridge above the ranch should bother him. With summer tourists hiking and camping all over the area, strangers were passing through all the time, their visits bringing income to the coffers of town merchants. Except for the occasional campfire burning out of control, they seldom posed a threat.

She chalked up Trace's uneasiness to the fact that he had lived too long in the Middle East with its ancient rivalries, suspicions and conflicts to accept the peaceful serenity of these Montana mountains at face value.

In spite of his newly acquired reserve, Trace was polite when they returned to the house after their ride. They discovered Mrs. Mac pushing Megan in a swing in the back yard. He gave the older woman and Megan a friendly greeting before launching into silence again.

"Have a nice ride?" her neighbor asked.

"Excellent," Cat replied. "How's Dad?"

"Still asleep. I made tuna salad and left it in the fridge for sandwiches for your lunch."

Cat saw Mrs. Mac off, awakened her father and went into the kitchen to prepare the midday meal. Trace remained outside with Megan, pushing her in the swing and catching her when she came down her sliding board, but as Cat observed them from the kitchen window, her chatty daughter did all the talking.

During lunch, Trace remained preoccupied until her father started talking about the upcoming graduation ceremonies at the high school.

"I'm sorry, sweetheart," her father said, "but I don't see how I can go tonight. If I take my pill, I won't be able to stay awake. If I don't take it, my sneezing and hacking will spoil the ceremony for everybody."

"But Grandpa," Megan said, "you hafta come and see me."

"You?" As if jolted from sleep, Trace looked at her daughter with surprise. "Aren't you a little young to graduate, short stuff?"

Megan puffed out her chest with pride. "I'm the mascot. They picked me. I get to wear a robe and hat—"

"Cap and gown," Cat corrected.

"—just like the big kids."

Trace's gaze met Cat's. "I didn't know senior classes had mascots nowadays."

"They decided to resurrect an old custom this year," Cat explained.

"Just for Megan," Gabe added, inflated with grandfatherly vanity. "The students have known her since she was a baby, and they want her to participate. I'm sorry I'll miss the graduation, Megan, but you can model your cap and gown for me before you go."

"Will you take my picture?" Megan asked coyly.

Cat laughed. "You know he will. Dad has albums full of photos from the day Megan was born."

"Really?" Trace gazed at Megan, that strange hunger shining in his eyes once again. "Can you show them to me?"

"Can I, Mommy?"

Cat couldn't believe their guest was really interested in Megan's photos, but she knew how much Megan enjoyed showing them off. "Are you through with your lunch?"

"Yes, ma'am."

"Then go wash your hands and bring your baby book down for Trace to see."

With a happy grin, Megan slid from her booster seat and headed upstairs.

Gabe waited until her footsteps sounded in the upstairs hall, then turned to Trace. "I have a favor to ask, young man."

"Ask away. You've been so kind to me, I'm glad for a chance to repay you."

Cat waited, puzzled over what her father had up his sleeve.

"I want you to escort my daughter and granddaughter to the graduation in town tonight."

"Oh, Dad, Trace will be bored to tears. He won't know a soul there."

"But I'd still enjoy it," Trace insisted. "I'd like to go. I can use a dose of good old Americana after so many years of foreign culture."

"If you really want to come," Cat said doubtfully, "you're welcome, but it isn't necessary for my sake."

Gabe, his expression somber, wiped his mouth and tossed his napkin onto his plate. "That's where you're wrong, Cat. It *is* necessary."

"Are you expecting trouble?" Trace asked.

"No," Cat insisted, frustrated by her father's overprotectiveness.

"Yes," Gabe answered at the same time.

Trace looked from one to the other. "Well?"

"Snake Larson," Gabe said, scowling, "the man who was here just before you arrived yesterday, may be in town tonight. If he's drinking, he'll be as ornery as a grizzly with a cub, and he's already shown more than a passing interest in my daughter. I don't want her and Megan facing him alone.''

''For Pete's sake,'' Cat said with a sigh of exasperation. ''Is Snake what you're worried about? He won't cause trouble. Everyone in town will be at the school tonight. We won't be alone.''

''Maybe so,'' her father said, ''but everyone in town won't be following you home up that deserted highway.''

Since Snake's first appearance at the ranch, Cat had kept a gun in a locked box at home and carried one in her car. And she knew when and how to use them.

''I can take care of myself—and Megan,'' Cat insisted.

''Of course you can,'' Trace said agreeably, ''but I'd like to come anyway, if you don't mind. I don't know the other students, but I'd enjoy watching Megan take part.''

Gabe looked pleased with himself, and Trace appeared so innocently cooperative that Cat had to squelch the impression she'd been manipulated. Besides, Trace was their guest, and since he'd expressed an interest in attending the graduation, refusing him would seem rude.

After lunch and time spent with Megan's album, Cat returned with Trace and Megan to the barn where they saddled up the pony and their horses. After a sedate ride down to the gate and back, Cat tucked Megan in for a nap. Megan begged to stay up with Trace, but Cat reminded her she'd be up past her bedtime that night and needed her rest. The clincher came when Cat warned that without a nap, Megan might fall asleep on stage during her mascot duties.

Her father, still groggy from his allergy pill, had completed a few chores before returning to bed for a nap. With the house quiet, Cat fixed tall glasses of iced tea and carried them to the front porch where Trace sat in the swing, staring at Preacher's Ridge, as if daring the morning's mysterious watcher to show himself.

She handed Trace a glass and sat beside him. "Dad has binoculars in the hall closet if you want them."

"No, thanks. I'm sure whoever was there this morning has moved on by now."

She settled back in the swing. "I appreciate how patient you were with Megan after lunch."

"Patient?"

"Letting her show you all those pictures."

His face lit up with a smile so brilliant, it had to be genuine. That kind of enthusiasm was hard to fake. "I enjoyed them. And I loved her stories. She talks about those times as if she can really remember them."

"She's heard Dad and me tell her about Marc and Ryan a hundred times. They're her favorite bedtime stories."

"She talks about Ryan as if she knows him."

"I want her to understand her father and be proud of who he was."

"A hero, she called him. Does she know what a hero is?"

"She knows her daddy and her uncle Marc saved the lives of nearly a hundred people, but she doesn't yet grasp the concept of their sacrifice. She will when she's older."

He finished his tea and set his glass aside. "Tell me about Marc. I was still in the hospital when they transferred him here. Was he aware that he'd come home?"

Her throat tightened with sadness. "I'm not sure. On fair days, we'd bring him out here in his wheelchair, and I can only hope he knew where he was."

"Seeing him like that must have been really tough on you and Gabe."

Understanding and compassion resonated in Trace's voice, and she appreciated having someone to talk to about those days when Marc lay in a coma, so unlike the strong and vibrant brother she remembered. Discussing Marc even now was too painful for her father, and not wanting to upset Gabe, Cat had kept all her feelings bottled up inside.

"One of the worst parts," she said, "was how helpless he was. Marc had always been so big and energetic and self-sufficient. I hope he wasn't aware of all we had to do for him. He would have hated it."

"Did he ever speak?"

She shook her head. "Sometimes he moaned and cried. Sometimes he laughed. The neurologist explained that those responses were reflexive and we shouldn't attach any meaning to them."

"That must have been hell for you, having to witness that." He slid his arm around her and squeezed her shoulder gently, and without thinking she settled easily into the solace of his embrace.

"Marc's incapacitation was hardest on Dad, and now, since I've had Megan, I understand why. For a parent to see his child suffering and not be able to help has to be the most awful feeling in the world."

"I'm sorry. I wish Marc had come out of his coma to talk to you both."

"Oh, but he did, right before he died."

Trace stiffened beside her. "He did?"

Cat nodded, fighting tears. "He opened his eyes. I was sitting beside the bed, and as clear as day, he said, 'Hi, Pest.' In that one instant, the Marc I'd known and loved was back. I ran to get Dad and Megan—she was only a few months old. When we returned, Marc told Dad and me how much he loved us. I showed him Megan and told him who she was. He asked for Ryan." Her voice broke. "But we didn't have the heart to tell him Ryan was...dead."

"Did he say anything else?"

She couldn't be certain, but Trace's voice sounded heavy with sorrow—and a hint of excitement. "He asked a question about Ryan, something that made no sense."

"What was it?"

"Oh, the words *seemed* clear enough. It sounded like, 'Did Ryan hit the button?' but the closest we could come to a meaning was that Marc wanted to know if Ryan had sounded the alarm at the embassy before the bombing."

"And that's all Marc said?"

"He lapsed into unconsciousness and died shortly after." She choked back a sob. "I miss him so much."

"I know." Trace pulled her against his chest and held her. His hand caressed her hair while he rocked them gently in the swing with the toe of his boot.

The tears she'd held back for so many years, trying to be strong for her father and not wanting to add to his pain, escaped in torrents, racking her body with sobs. The more she tried to staunch them, the harder she cried.

With amazing gentleness, Trace held her, soothed her and let her cry.

When her tears were finally spent, she pulled back, embarrassed by her display, horrified to see that her tears had left a huge damp splotch on the front of his shirt.

"You must think I'm an emotional fool," she said.

With a tender smile and a shake of his head, he pulled a fresh handkerchief from the pocket of his jeans and handed it to her. "I think you're a woman who loved her brother and misses him."

She wiped her eyes and blew her nose. "I'm sorry about your shirt."

"It'll dry."

He still had his arm around her, and when she looked at him, the warmth of his expression eased her pain. He lifted his hand, and she turned her face into it.

His palm cradled her cheek. "You're a remarkable woman, Cat Erickson."

Before she realized what was happening, he had bent down until his lips touched hers, soft and consoling. She gasped in surprise, breathing in the distinctive masculine scent of him. He tasted of lemony iced tea, yet provocatively male. Her lips opened beneath his, and she leaned toward him, sliding her arms around his neck, yielding to the longing she'd experienced inexplicably since she'd met him.

Pulling her to him, he threaded his fingers through her hair. Unresisting, she surrendered and molded her body to his. Her breasts crushed against the hard muscles of his chest, and she could feel his heart hammering against her blouse and the heat of him seeping through the dense fabric of her jeans. Long buried emotions and stifled longings roused and stirred within her, and she reveled in the heady sensation of being alive, a feeling she hadn't experienced since she'd lost Ryan.

Had she lost her mind, as well?

As if struggling to surface from deep water, with the flat of her palms she pushed herself away and returned to her side of the swing. Confusion and alarm overwhelmed her, and more heat, not of passion this time but of embarrassment, surged up her neck and flamed into her cheeks. She forced herself to meet his steady gaze.

Trace's greenish-brown eyes appeared smoky with desire, but his words were contrite. "Sorry. I shouldn't have—"

"No apologies needed." The words tumbled out sharper than she'd intended.

That she could present such an unaffected attitude amazed her, since her emotions were a seething cauldron of desire. She stood on slightly wobbly legs, feeling as weak as a newborn foal, and straightened her clothes.

She edged closer to the door, beyond his reach, more to remove herself from temptation than from expecting him to reach for her. "You were only being kind."

A slight smile quirked the corner of his wide, delectable mouth. "Is that what you think?"

She shrugged, pretending nonchalance, while her rebellious heart fluttered. "What else could it be when a woman blubbers all over your shirt?"

"It may have started out as comfort—"

"Don't explain," she begged.

"Why?"

"Because…"

She couldn't think of a logical excuse to resist him, so she grabbed the first reason that came into her head.

"Because I'm still in love with Ryan. I'll always be in love with Ryan."

She didn't wait for his reaction. Turning on her heel, she fled inside and bounded up the stairs to her room.

Chapter Seven

Trace watched her go, stung by the irony that he was competing against himself for Cat's affection. He shouldn't have kissed her. He had pushed her too far, too fast. Of course she'd drawn back. His practical, down-to-earth Cat would never commit her heart to a stranger, even if the attraction between them was undeniable. She'd loved Ryan for years before she'd given him a clue to her real feelings.

He shouldn't have kissed her at all. Until he could tell her who he was, he had no right. But now that he had kissed her once and realized how much his memories had dimmed compared to the reality of Cat in his arms, her lips against his, the taste of her more delicious than he had recalled, how could he stand not kissing her again?

He sighed. He probably wouldn't remain at High Valley Ranch long enough to get another chance—or for Cat to admit she was drawn to him. He'd already discovered what he'd come for. Before he died, Marc had said nothing of any significance to Wentworth's investigation. And Trace's repressed memories showed no sign of returning. The colonel would have to look elsewhere for a clue to finding Righteous Sword.

And in a day or two, Trace Gallagher would leave High Valley Ranch forever.

HOURS LATER, in the summer twilight, Cat parked the car in the high school lot and unstrapped Megan from her car seat. Trace climbed out of the passenger side.

"The ceremony won't start for another hour," she explained in the brisk, impersonal manner she'd adopted since their kiss earlier on the porch, "but I have to issue the seniors their caps and gowns."

"And I get to help," Megan said. "Mommy promised."

He grinned at his daughter. "I'm sure she's counting on it."

"You'll be on your own," Cat told him, "until the ceremony starts, unless you want to hang out here. There're probably magazines in the library—"

"Don't worry about me," Trace said. "I can walk downtown and still be back in plenty of time." He scanned the parking lot and noted a few other cars. "You won't be by yourself in there?"

Cat shook her head. "Todd Brewster, the principal, and several faculty members are already here, and the others will arrive soon. We'll be fine."

"I promised your father—"

"Dad worries too much. Always has, but he's been worse since Marc died. Do some sight-seeing. I'll meet you here at the car after the ceremony."

Trace watched until Cat and Megan were safely inside before he turned toward downtown. He could have walked the whole area blindfolded and still known his way. The same prim, Victorian houses lined the streets, lawns neatly mowed and flowers blooming in perennial borders with the small-town charm he remembered.

Through undrawn curtains, he spotted one family enjoying a late supper around the kitchen table. Passing another house, he glimpsed a lighted living room with the father reading a newspaper, the mother with a baby on her lap and two children in front of the television, watching "Wheel of Fortune."

The sights filled him with longing. Except for the few years he'd lived in Margaret Sweeney's foster home, he'd never had a real home, never belonged anywhere. In the Marine Corps he'd lived in foreign lands, uncovered plots and conspiracies, experienced danger, lost his best friend and several buddies and almost forfeited his life. It had been exciting at the time, but he'd had enough. All he wanted now was a place of his own, with Megan on his lap and Cat at his side. Even such a mundane activity as watching a TV game show held a seductive charm, if Cat and Megan were there.

He shook off his yearnings. The terrorist bomb had spoiled his plans for establishing his home and family at High Valley Ranch with Cat anytime soon—plans his injuries had wiped totally from his mind until a few weeks ago.

That thought reminded him that he needed to report

to Colonel Wentworth, and if his present memory served, the supermarket had a pay phone out front he could use. Trace had requested a cell phone for this mission, but Wentworth had warned against it. "Too easily monitored," he'd explained, "and unreliable reception in the mountains."

When Trace reached the store, its front door sported a sign that read Closed for Graduation, but the pay phone he'd recalled was by the entrance. He punched in the toll-free number Wentworth had made him memorize.

"Wentworth," the colonel answered on the first ring.

"It's Gallagher."

"Tell me some good news."

"I wish I could, sir. According to his sister, Erickson said nothing that would help us."

The colonel's sigh reverberated in his ear. "I was afraid of that."

"Shall I return to Washington?"

"Any sign of those memories returning?"

"Nothing yet, sir."

"You haven't been there long. Can you stay a while without raising suspicions?"

"I can try, but I really don't see what good—"

"Getting your memory back is our best shot. I want you in Athens, preferably at the ranch if you can swing it, until I say otherwise. That's an order."

"Yes, sir."

Abruptly the line went dead.

A glance at his watch told Trace he still had thirty

minutes before the program began at the high school. He ambled down the boardwalk to the nearest saloon, where he and Marc had shot pool and guzzled cold beers on their last leave. Only one battered truck was parked out front, and he found the saloon almost empty. After ordering a beer at the bar, he moved to a table in a dim corner.

In the back of the room, three men were playing pool, and Trace recognized Snake Larson. He'd bulked up since Trace last saw him, and his pugnacious appearance had grown coarser with age. Glad that Snake was downtown and not at the high school causing trouble, Trace finished his drink and left the three arguing over whether Snake's foot had left the floor during a shot.

The parking lot was overflowing when Trace returned to the high school, and the only seat he could find in the crowded auditorium was in the next to the last row. He settled into it just in time for the first strains of "Pomp and Circumstance."

When he caught sight of Megan, dressed in a tiny navy-blue gown and matching mortarboard with tassel and leading the senior class down the aisle, his throat tightened, his eyes stung and his heart thumped like consecutive mortar fire. Assisted by two members of the graduating class, she clambered up the steps to the stage while the rest of the class filed into the front rows of the auditorium.

Onstage, Cat stepped out from the wings with other faculty members and the principal Trace had met the previous day. Catching sight of her mother, Megan's face lit up like a spotlight. She wiggled her fingers and grinned happily, and Cat, her pride in her daughter written all over her beautiful face, returned her wave.

The last senior took his seat, and the music died. The principal stepped to the lectern to issue a welcome and introduce the senior class president, but Trace's attention was on Cat and his daughter. Happiness and pride consumed him. He'd missed too many milestones in their lives, and he was thankful to share this one.

He would always regret that he hadn't been there when Cat went into labor and Megan was born. He hadn't been around to help with the two o'clock feedings, to change dirty diapers, or to walk the floor with Megan when she had colic. He hadn't witnessed her first steps, heard her first words. He hadn't been there to dry her tears when she scraped her knee. He'd been robbed of watching her first sight of a Christmas tree, her first pony ride, and he'd been cheated of sharing all these experiences with Cat, the woman he loved more than life.

His head throbbed with anger at the terrorists who had stolen so much from him, and he wished he could tap the memory that identified them. He *had* to remember, for himself and Cat and Marc and for ninety-eight other people who would never see their loved ones again. Remembering the psychiatrist's advice, he forced himself to relax. His memories would return faster without coercion, the doctor had promised, but Trace wasn't so sure. Weeks after the majority of his amnesia had disappeared, he had yet to recall anything other than what had come back that first day when he'd bumped his head.

He turned his attention to the stage, where Cat was assisting the principal in handing out diplomas as the seniors trekked across the stage. In a trim navy-blue suit, white silk blouse and high-heeled shoes that called attention to her long, slender legs and trim ankles, Cat didn't look much older than her students, but Trace could measure their respect for her in the way they shook her hand and accepted her congratulations.

When the ceremony ended, Trace noted the students weren't the only ones fond of Cat. The principal escorted her to her seat with a too-warm smile and a possessive hand at the small of her back.

"See that?" a woman behind him whispered loudly to the man next to her. "I'll bet this time next year Miss Erickson is married to Mr. Brewster."

"That's old news," he replied.

Their words jolted Trace. Before he'd returned to Cat, he'd considered she might have found someone else, but seeing her again had wiped those thoughts from his mind. Now, however, watching her laugh and chat with Brewster, her face aglow with happiness, Trace wondered at the depth of her relationship with the principal. To Cat, Trace was only a stranger passing through. She had no reason to share her affairs, her affections or her plans for the future with him.

No reason to know how much he loved her.

For the first time, he considered the possibility that revealing his identity even once the terrorist danger had passed might be a mistake. If Cat had forged a new life without him, what right did he have after so many years to reappear and turn it upside down?

"YOU'RE AWFULLY quiet," Cat remarked on the drive home. "I hope you weren't too bored tonight."

Trace jerked himself from his thoughts. The possibility that Cat might be in love with Todd Brewster rankled him. Even while admitting the irrationality of his response, he felt betrayed and bereft. After all, he reminded himself, Ryan had been dead to Cat for years. Going on with her life was the natural and healthy thing to do.

Especially with regard to Megan, fast asleep in her car seat in the back.

"I was thinking of all those seniors," he improvised, "and the shock they're in for when they hit the real world."

"We try to prepare them," Cat said, "but high school's nothing like the cold, hard reality of being on your own for the first time in your life."

"Your principal seems like a nice guy."

"He's terrific. It took a while for the school and the town to warm up to him. A small place like this is usually suspicious of strangers—" She broke off with an embarrassed laugh. "Present company excepted, of course."

Her voice had warmed significantly when she spoke of Brewster, but Trace had no way of gauging the depth of her feelings. He decided to give it a try anyway.

"So you're fond of Brewster."

"Very." She cut a glance at him from the corner of her eye. "But not the way I think you mean."

"What do you think I mean?"

"That I'm in love with him."

"Are you?"

She hesitated so long his heart plummeted in his chest. "He wants me to marry him."

God, it was worse than he thought. "And what do you want?"

She shrugged. "I lost what I wanted five years ago. Now it's Dad and especially Megan I need to worry about."

"What do they have to do with Brewster?"

"Todd could help Dad at the ranch before and after school during the term and full-time in summer. And he'd make a terrific father for Megan. He's really good with children."

He felt sick inside, as if someone had died, at the thought of another man raising his daughter. "Sounds like you've made up your mind."

She shook her head. "My head tells me accepting would be the smart thing to do, but my heart—"

Flustered, she glanced at him again, and even by the dim lights from the dashboard, he could see the flush creeping over her face.

"What does your heart tell you?"

Gripping the wheel, she stared straight ahead. "That I don't love Todd the way I loved Ryan."

Her words were faint consolation, since she believed Ryan dead.

They drove a few more miles in silence before she turned to him again. "You're an objective observer. What would you advise?"

Stop the car and let me kiss you again the way I did this afternoon.

"Hey." He worked at keeping his tone light. "You can call in the Marines for all kinds of help, but for this job, you should ask Dear Abby. Matters of the heart are out of my league."

"You don't have someone you care about?"

If you only knew.

"I had to be careful in Tabari. If I looked at one of their women the wrong way, I could have found myself dead very quickly." Frustrated by the direction of the conversation, he changed the subject. "Megan did a great job tonight."

"She loves the attention," Cat said. "It's so lonely for her on the ranch with just Dad and me, I think it's good for her to—"

They had reached the entrance to the ranch, and Cat stopped the car.

"What's the matter?" Trace asked.

"The gate's open. We closed it when we left."

"Maybe the MacIntoshes dropped in to check on your dad."

"Not this late. They're dairy farmers, remember? Their day begins at four o'clock, so they went to bed hours ago." Cat shook her head with a worried frown.

"Maybe the catch wasn't fastened, so the wind blew the gate open."

"I made certain it was latched tight when I closed it." Trace remembered how he'd tested the catch with a strong tug before climbing into the car at their departure.

With a puzzled frown, Cat eased the car through the gate and up the road toward the house. "I'm probably worrying for nothing. Maybe a visitor Dad wasn't expecting left it open."

Trace said nothing, but he was on full alert. Everyone in Athens had been at the graduation tonight.

Except Snake Larson and his cronies.

"Turn off your headlights," Trace said at the final bend before the house. "There's enough moonlight to show the way. And go slow."

After an anxious glance at Megan, still sleeping soundly in the back seat, Cat did as he asked. The big SUV glided silently toward the ranch house, the only sound the faint crunch of gravel beneath the tires. When they reached the house, moonlight illuminated the dark bulk of a pickup truck parked by the front walk.

"Recognize the vehicle?" Trace asked.

Cat shook her head and pulled her SUV in behind it.

Lights blazed from all the windows, and the sounds of breaking glass and splintering wood floated toward them on the night breeze.

Trace spotted the dark shadows of at least three men outlined against the curtains as they moved through the house. From the violence of their actions, Trace could tell this was no friendly visit.

"Daddy's in there!" Cat cried.

"I'll take care of Gabe." He reached for the door handle. "You keep Megan safe. Call the sheriff on your cell phone and take Megan to the MacIntosh farm. Now!"

He jumped from the car and ran up the front walk toward the house.

Chapter Eight

Trace halted at the porch steps and turned to watch Cat's SUV disappear down the drive. If he went barging in now, he would roust the intruders on her heels. He didn't want to risk their forcing her off the narrow highway in their haste to escape.

Unfortunately, their escape was probably the best scenario he could hope for.

He'd counted at least three men inside. If they were armed, even with his superior hand-to-hand combat training he was definitely outmatched. His main concern was for Gabe. Trace decided to leave apprehending the home invaders to the law. If he could drive the intruders from the house, they had only one road out of the area, the same road the sheriff would travel to reach High Valley. With any luck, the lawman and his deputies would intercept the criminals if Trace could somehow convince them to leave.

While Trace debated the best method to evict them, the clamor inside the house lessened, and he heard a deep voice call, "Find anything?"

"Zip," a rough voice answered from a different room.

"I've got something." A third voice sounded from upstairs. "Let's get the hell outta here."

There was a thud of heavy boots descending the interior staircase, and Trace managed to duck around the side of the house before the screen door slammed open. Three large figures jumped from the porch and bolted to the pickup truck. The driver had the engine started and in gear before the third man closed the passenger door. With the motor roaring and its heavy tires spewing gravel, the truck circled and headed down the drive toward the entrance at high speed.

Once their taillights disappeared, Trace darted inside. The intruders had left the lights burning, and the sight of their destruction stunned him. Drawers had been pulled open, their contents dumped, furniture upended, knickknacks shattered, rugs thrown back. A hurried search of the first floor revealed no sign of Gabe.

"Gabe!" Trace shouted. "Where are you?"

In the stillness, a soft moan floated down the stairs. Trace took the steps to the second floor three at a time. The same devastation had been wreaked on the second floor, and he had to jump over debris to reach Gabe's bedroom. When he crossed the threshold, Gabe's bed was empty, and the spacious room appeared unoccupied.

A groan sounded from the far side of the room.

Rounding the bed, Trace spotted Gabe slumped in the corner.

The older man was struggling to rise. One arm hung limply at his side.

"Take it easy." Trace hurried to him. "I'll help."

Sliding an arm beneath the shoulder of Gabe's good arm, he assisted him to the bed and eased him to a sitting position against the headboard. "What happened?"

Dazed, Gabe shook his head. "One minute I was asleep. The next a bright light's shining in my face. I jumped out of bed and tried to fight them, but someone grabbed me. A big guy wearing a ski mask and gloves flung me in that corner. I must have passed out, because the next thing I knew, you were shouting my name downstairs."

Trace noted the knot forming above Gabe's eye. "You hit your head. And it looks as if your arm's broken. Is there a phone upstairs?"

"In Cat's room. You calling the sheriff?"

"Cat's already called him."

"I don't want Megan to see me like this."

"Cat and Megan are on their way to the Mac-Intoshes. The intruders were still here when we returned from town, so I wanted her and Megan safely out of their way."

"Could you see who they were?"

Trace shook his head. "Like you said, they wore ski masks, dark clothes and gloves. Will you be okay while I call an ambulance?"

With a stubborn set to his jaw, Gabe attempted to stand. "I don't need an ambulance."

With a firm but gentle shove, Trace pushed him

onto the bed. "You need that arm set and you could have a concussion. Now stay put until I get back."

In Cat's room, he found the phone slung under the bed but still working. While placing the call for an ambulance, he surveyed the damage. Her room, too, had been thoroughly trashed. Had the men been looking for money and valuables? He remembered the watcher on the ridge earlier that day and wondered if, despite Cat's skepticism, someone had been casing the house in preparation for the night's break-in.

But why?

Cat had assured him the only items of value on the ranch were the cattle. Had the robbers struck because of the isolated locale, figuring to get in and out so easily that it didn't matter if their take was small?

After the operator assured him that medical assistance was on the way, Trace quickly inspected the rest of the second floor. Every room, including Megan's and Marc's, had been tossed, and when he reached the guest room, he found his belongings strewn across the floor. The contents of his shaving kit had been dumped in the guest bathroom.

He returned to Gabe, who had propped himself against the headboard, his face ashen, his right arm clutched awkwardly against his side.

"The paramedics will be here soon," Trace said. "Are you in much pain?"

Gabe shook his head in denial, but his gray pallor said otherwise. "But I'm mad as hell. Who would do this?"

"Cat and I saw someone watching the ranch from

Preacher's Ridge this morning. Maybe they were drifters, passing through and looking for some easy cash.''

Gabe's eyes narrowed thoughtfully. "Or Snake Larson and his friends.''

"I saw them drinking in town earlier tonight.'' *Three of them,* Trace recalled.

Gabe nodded knowingly. "Snake's a coward. He would have figured the whole family would attend the graduation. Everyone in town knew Megan was the class mascot. He said he'd get even with me for running him off. Must have been surprised to find me here asleep.''

Out front, a vehicle approached and braked quickly. Car doors slammed.

"The sheriff couldn't get here that fast,'' Gabe warned. "The thugs may have come back. Look behind the panel in the middle of the top closet shelf. I keep a loaded handgun there so Megan can't find it.''

Trace was headed for the closet when Cat's voice called from downstairs. "Daddy? Trace?''

"We're up here,'' Trace shouted.

Seconds later, Cat hurried into the room, her face flushed, her hair wind-tossed. She rushed to her father. "Are you all right?''

"Broken arm,'' Trace warned her when she reached to hug her dad. "Paramedics are on the way. Where's Megan? She shouldn't see all this.''

Cat eased onto the bed beside her father and took his hand. "After contacting the sheriff, I called the MacIntoshes, and they met me halfway. Mrs. Mac took Megan to the farm, and Mr. Mac and his sons came with me. They're downstairs.''

Trace considered Gabe's worsening color. ''We'll take your father to meet the paramedics. That way he'll get treatment quicker. Mr. Mac and his boys can wait here for the sheriff.''

Gabe didn't argue. He attempted to stand, but his knees gave way beneath him, and he sank onto the bed. Trace rigged a makeshift splint to stabilize Gabe's arm, and the older man didn't object when Trace scooped him up in his arms and carried him downstairs to the car.

After settling Gabe on the back seat, Trace climbed in beside Cat, and she headed the car down the mountain.

She nodded to her cell phone in the well between the seats. ''Better call the paramedics. Tell them to watch out for us on the road.''

While Cat drove, Trace placed the call, then turned to check on Gabe. ''Try to stay awake,'' he warned him, ''just in case you have a concussion.''

''I'm too damned mad to sleep,'' came the irascible reply.

Trace glanced at Cat, her face illuminated by the glow of the dash lights. Her brow was slightly furrowed as she concentrated on the dark, winding road, but her courage and determination were unmistakable. Other women might have gone to pieces in a similar situation, but not Cat. Adversity apparently brought out the best in her.

The question of who had caused the trouble niggled

at Trace. He hoped to God Gabe was right, that the intruders had been Snake and his pals. Trace could even accept the desperate-drifters-looking-for-cash theory.

What he didn't want to contemplate was the possibility that his presence at the ranch was connected to the break-in. If someone was interested in Trace Gallagher and what he was doing at High Valley, they were all in serious trouble.

EARLY THE NEXT MORNING, Cat stepped out the kitchen door into the swirling mist. Although the sun had been up for hours, it served only to brighten the low cloud cover to a dull gray. She'd slept a couple of hours after the sheriff and his deputies had left, but in spite of her exhaustion, she'd awakened at her usual time and couldn't go back to sleep.

Longing for coffee but unable to face the disorder the intruders had left in the kitchen, she tromped across the yard. The mist obscured the way, and she followed the familiar route by instinct. After feeding the chickens and taking care of the horses, still unready to tackle the disaster in the house, she settled onto a bale of hay next to Rogue's stall and leaned against the door. The horse snuffled companionably, and she took comfort in his presence.

In a little while she would call the hospital to check on her father. As soon as he'd been admitted, Gabe had started insisting that they return to High Valley to assist in the sheriff's investigation, but she and Trace had waited for results of the doctor's initial examination. Dr. Wright had diagnosed Gabe's slight concussion and claimed that the break in his arm was clean and should heal easily. She'd recommended that Gabe stay at least twenty-four hours for observation.

To Cat's surprise, her father had agreed without protest. She worried that he had acquiesced too quickly to a prolonged stay. Her main worry was that the home invasion had broken his spirit, already bruised by the loss of his boys and his financial worries about the ranch.

"You're either up early or asleep with your eyes open." A rich, husky voice intruded on her thoughts.

Startled, Cat glanced up to find Trace, holding a mug of steaming coffee in each hand, standing in front of her. In spite of the early hour and his lack of sleep, his hazel eyes appraised her with surprising clarity. Comfortable and at ease in his jeans, chambray shirt and denim jacket, he looked as if he'd dressed that way all his life. He smelled pleasantly of soap, the strong line of his jaw was freshly shaved, and his thick hair was slightly damp from the shower.

Her heart lifted and did a strange and unmistakable flip-flop at the sight of him, and the dismal day suddenly seemed brighter.

"One of those coffees better be for me," she said with pretended fierceness, "or I may have to turn violent."

"There's been enough violence around here already." He handed her a cup, stroked Rogue's muzzle, then sat beside her on the bale. "You seemed a thousand miles away."

Reflecting on how agreeable sharing her morning coffee with him was, she took a deep swallow. "I was just thinking how lucky we are that spring roundup is already over. The calves have been cut out and sold, and the cattle that needed veterinary care have been tended to. Dad couldn't handle any of that now with a broken arm."

"You're still going to need help."

"I'll have to hire someone." Calculating the additional withdrawal from her already dwindling funds, she sighed.

"What about me?"

"Hire you?" she sputtered in surprise.

"Not hire," he said with a shake of his head and a grin that chased away the morning's gloom. "I'm too inexperienced for you to pay me. But I have several days of leave left, I know horses and I'm strong enough to do grunt work."

The prospect of his remaining longer at the ranch was very appealing, but she shook her head. "You're on vacation. I couldn't ask you to stay here and work when you could be off having fun."

"You think of this as work." He waved his hand to encompass the barn and beyond. "To someone like me, it's an adventure. But if you'd rather hire someone more experienced—"

"No!"

Her too quick and too emphatic response flustered her, reminding her of the lie she'd told Trace the night before. She'd insisted that she'd never love anyone the way she'd loved Ryan, but each time she encountered this handsome stranger, her reactions and responses were almost as strong and unsettling as her feelings toward Ryan had been.

Not that she loved Trace, she assured herself. How could she, when she'd known him only a few days? But the chemistry between them was undeniable, and she had no doubt that with time, the magnetism could grow into something deeper. She felt as if the two of them were caught in a centrifugal force that spun them closer and closer together.

For that reason alone, extending his stay wasn't a good idea. She was convinced that the longer they were together, the more she'd grow to like him. Liking him, even loving him, wouldn't be a problem if he wasn't a Marine who had to spend most of his time in dangerous situations on the other side of the world. She couldn't face loving and losing again.

She glanced up to find Trace studying her with a contemplative look.

"Having second thoughts?" he asked.

"About what?" For a moment she feared he'd read her mind, then realized he was still talking about working the ranch.

"Having me around. Considering what happened last night, maybe you think I'm bad luck."

Recalling the home invasion clinched her decision. Trace's steady presence in a crisis had been a godsend. With her dad incapacitated, until the intruders were caught she'd feel much safer with a combat-trained Marine under her roof. She was a big girl, after all, and could guard her feelings for a few days in exchange for the security and assistance Trace was offering.

"If you're willing to work for room and board," she conceded, "I'm glad to have you."

He nodded with apparent satisfaction. "That's settled then. And speaking of board, how about some breakfast?"

She groaned and slumped where she sat. "I'm starving, but I can't face what they did to the kitchen."

"No need to." He stood, grabbed her hand and tugged her to her feet. "I cleaned up most of it while the coffee was brewing. And I'm volunteering to cook."

She laughed. "If I'd known cooking was part of the deal, I'd have offered you a permanent job."

"We can always renegotiate my contract." With a nonchalance that made the gesture seem routine, he placed his arm around her shoulders, and they walked to the house.

THIRTY MINUTES LATER, Cat returned to the kitchen after placing calls to check on her father and Megan. She halted in surprise on the threshold. The shattered crockery had been swept from the floor, drawers replaced in the cabinets, their contents restored. Sugar and flour the intruders had spilled from their canisters had been wiped away, and the entire kitchen sparkled.

"You've worked wonders," she said.

"Just a little leatherneck spit and polish," he said with a smile. "I aim to please."

''Pleased isn't the word. I'm astounded.''

Trace had set the table with a yellow-checkered cloth and her mother's Blue Willow dishes, which had somehow survived the previous night's rampage. Cat was grateful they'd come through unscathed. Their sentimental value made them irreplaceable.

At Cat's place was a plate heaped with fluffy French toast and crisp bacon, accompanied by a glass of orange juice, a fresh cup of coffee and a pitcher of warm huckleberry syrup.

She could get used to this, she thought. Breakfast served by an attractive and companionable man. And that attitude was a problem. As long as Trace was around, she had to keep reminding herself his presence was merely temporary. She had no reason, however, not to appreciate his competence and helpfulness while he was here.

She took her seat. ''You certainly know your way around a kitchen.''

''It's a great place.'' Trace sat across from her, then glanced around the room, the strong lines of his face softened by nostalgia. ''The heart of the home. Isn't that what designers call it?''

She wondered if he was homesick for his mother's kitchen in Syracuse. ''Do you still own your family's home in New York?''

He gazed at her blankly for a moment, then blinked rapidly. ''No, I sold the house after they died.''

His obviously uncomfortable reaction to her question made her change the subject. ''I spoke with Dad's doctor.''

"Can he come home today?"

She shook her head and attempted to tamp down her concern. "Dr. Wright wants to keep him a while longer. His blood pressure spiked during the night. She thinks it's probably a delayed reaction to the break-in, but she wants him under observation, just to be certain."

"Your father has a fighting spirit." Trace's voice was calm, a soothing balm to her troubled mind. "Attitude's half the battle. I'm betting he'll be feeling better and on his way home soon."

She took a bite of French toast, which tasted as good as it looked and smelled. "Mrs. Mac suggested Megan stay at least until tomorrow."

Trace nodded. "Maybe Gabe will be back by then. And her extended stay gives us time to clean up the place before she comes home. She wouldn't understand what's happened. Hell, I don't understand it."

Just another trait to like about the man, she thought. He cared about her daughter's welfare. And his use of the word "us" made Cat feel less alone and overwhelmed by the chaos the intruders had inflicted on her home.

"Will Megan be homesick?" he asked.

"Mrs. Mac's oldest son has a daughter Megan's age, plus she told me this morning that one of the barn cats has a new litter of kittens. Megan will have the time of her life. I may have to drag her away when the time comes."

He grinned. "She may arrive home with one of those kittens. Would you mind?"

Cat shook her head. "What's one more animal when we have so many?"

They dug into their breakfast in companionable silence. As they were eating, Cat remembered something from earlier that morning that had been puzzling her.

"Why," she asked Trace, "were you so adamant that the deputies not dust for fingerprints?"

A strained look flitted across his face. Guilt? Surprise? It was gone before she could identify it.

"Both your father and I noticed that the intruders wore gloves." He reached for the pitcher and drizzled more syrup on his toast. "Have you ever seen the mess technicians make when they dust for prints?"

She shook her head.

"Believe me," he said, "picking up after the jerks who broke in will be enough of a chore without having to clean fingerprint chemicals, too."

Slightly in awe, she gazed at him. Maybe his Marine training had him better prepared to deal with the unexpected, but she'd never have thought in a million years to object to the unnecessary fingerprinting.

"What I don't understand," Trace said between mouthfuls, "is why the sheriff didn't meet the intruders on the highway. Your dad said it's the only way in and out of here."

"The highway's the only paved road, but an entire network of logging roads run off it and crisscross through the mountains. The men who broke in could have pulled onto one of those roads long enough for the sheriff to pass."

Trace seemed lost in thought for a moment before he spoke again. "Would Snake Larson be familiar with those roads?"

She nodded. "He's worked on Forest Service brush crews since he was in high school. He knows the whole county as well as anyone."

"Gabe seems convinced the break-in was Snake's doing."

"I agree," Cat said. "Otherwise, it makes no sense."

He cocked an eyebrow in question. "How come?"

"Nothing was taken. Mom's sterling silver flatware, the cash in Dad's wallet. Seems like all they were interested in was wreaking havoc—right up Snake's alley."

Trace frowned but said nothing.

"You don't agree?" Cat asked.

He shrugged, and his expression remained troubled. "I don't know this Snake guy, so I can't form an opinion about his motives. But there is another explanation for nothing being stolen."

"Our arrival scared them off?"

His frown melted into an admiring grin. "You read my mind."

His approval pleased her—too much. And the smile on his lips reminded her of the kiss they'd shared yesterday. A kiss that had touched her more than she wanted to admit. A kiss that could prove deliciously addictive. So addictive, in fact, that she had to guard against it being repeated, even though at this very moment, all she wanted to do was leave her place at the table, perch on his lap and kiss him senseless.

She wanted him like a thirsty woman craves water.

Just like she'd wanted Ryan.

With a flush of embarrassment, she struggled to tame her rebellious feelings. After a few days, Trace would be gone, probably for good. She couldn't allow herself to indulge in emotional entanglements that led nowhere. She wanted to be able to say goodbye with a light heart and no regrets.

"I hope you can't read *my* mind," she said cryptically and avoided his curious gaze as she stood to clear the table.

"LET'S START in Megan's room," Trace said after breakfast. "If she decides to come home early, at least her space will be the way she's used to."

Besides his concern for Megan, he had another good reason for wanting to start on the second floor. Last night, he'd heard one of the intruders yell from upstairs that he'd found something. If Cat could determine what was missing, they might have a better chance of identifying the culprits.

Gabe and Cat believed Snake and his pals were responsible, and Trace hoped they were right. They should know soon enough. When the sheriff and his deputies had left in the wee hours before dawn, they were headed back to town to find Snake and check his alibi.

The fingerprint issue had been a close call. Fortunately, the intruders had worn gloves, as Trace and

Gabe had seen. Otherwise, the crime techs would have dusted for prints—and Trace would have faced the problem of explaining why the fingerprints of Ryan Christopher, a dead man, were all over the house.

"Choose your weapon," Cat said, interrupting his musings. She held a broom in one hand and a mop in the other.

"I'll take both. This campaign requires a full-scale assault."

She responded with a cocky salute and a saucy sparkle in her blue eyes that almost undid his resolve to keep his distance.

"You're in charge of the heavy guns," she said. "I'll manage the light artillery."

She opened the cabinet beneath the sink and knelt before it, pulling out a bucket, dust cloths and cleaning solutions. Reaching for something in the back of the cupboard, she leaned forward, thrusting her well-formed bottom, encased in smooth denim, into the air with an unintentional but extremely provocative wiggle.

Desire stabbed through him like a Marine dress saber, and his palms itched with the memory of her bottom cupped in his hands while sunlight filtered through the trees of the glade and bathed their naked bodies like a blessing. Calling on all the discipline the Corps had instilled in him, he shoved the cherished memory away. His task would be so much easier if, instead of forgetting who'd bombed the embassy, he'd forgotten loving Cat.

Forget loving Cat? Who was he kidding?

He'd give his right arm before he'd relinquish recollections of their lovemaking. If his suppressed memories didn't surface, those cherished reminiscences might be all he had left of his life with Cat.

She likes Trace Gallagher, an inner voice taunted him. *Trace could win her heart if Ryan can't return.*

The possibility was enticing, but Trace rejected it on the spot. Unless he could somehow dredge up the terrorist's name from his subconscious or Wentworth could track down Righteous Sword without Trace's help, Ryan Christopher would remain buried forever in the family plot on the hill above the ranch. And Trace Gallagher would disappear in order to keep Cat and Megan safe from terrorist attention.

Trace had initially balked at the idea that Ryan's existence put the Ericksons in danger, but Wentworth had driven home the truth of it with gruesome clarity. "The main reason we haven't caught these bastards," Wentworth insisted, "is their attention to detail. Every time we caught the faintest lead, we'd arrive to question a suspect only to find him and his entire family butchered. Righteous Sword is relentless about not leaving a trail."

"Why should they think Ryan a threat?"

"Word of Marc's dying statement, that Ryan knew who'd shot him, spread through the embassy personnel like wildfire. Since the terrorist had a man inside, it's a cinch they know that Ryan knew who at least one of them was." Wentworth had leaned forward across his desk, his expression grim. "I'm telling you that if Ryan surfaces before they're caught, the terrorists will know, and they'll kill everyone close to him.''

Trace suppressed a shudder. As much as he wanted Cat, he couldn't place her in danger by revealing his true identity.

"All set?" Cat had loaded her supplies in the bucket and stood watching him with a puzzled look.

He shook his gloomy thoughts away and forced a smile. "Lead the way."

A moment later, he wished he'd taken point instead. Following her up the stairs brought its own special torture. She moved with a grace that managed to appear both efficient and languid, and her unique honeysuckle scent enveloped him in her wake. His best plan was to work up a sweat quickly to provide an excuse for a cold shower.

As they tackled the debacle in Megan's room, however, his exertions eased the pain of his desire. With military efficiency, he swept up potting mix scattered from a trailing ivy, then repotted the plant. While he worked, Cat gathered Megan's toys, which had been strewn around the room and under the bed.

"Oh, no," she cried.

He set the plant on the dresser and turned to her. "What is it?"

She dangled a bedraggled Pooh Bear between her fingers, its left arm hanging by a thread. "Next to Teddy, this is Megan's favorite."

"Get me a needle and thread. I'll fix it."

She fixed him with an incredulous stare. "You sew?"

"Doesn't everyone?"

She shook her head and studied him with an intense scrutiny that made him shift uneasily beneath her laser gaze. Suddenly her eyes widened and her mouth formed an O. "You're not Trace Gallagher!"

Panic seized him as all his good intentions washed down the drain. He should have known that Cat would recognize him, even after all these years, in spite of his altered voice and appearance.

"I know who you are," she insisted.

"Who?" He forced the words through a mouth gone dry with fear and regret.

A smile tugged at the corners of her mouth, and mischief flickered in her eyes. "He cooks. He cleans. He sews." She nodded emphatically. "You're Martha Stewart in disguise."

He laughed to cover the tremendous sigh of relief that whooshed from his lungs. "Marines learn to take care of themselves. It's a good thing."

She laughed, too, and he was glad to see her lovely face lose the pinched, wan look she'd worn all morning.

"I'll get the sewing kit," she said.

"Where does this plant go?"

"On the table by Megan's bed. Next to Ryan's pictures."

Cat left the room, and Trace moved to the bedside where a frame lay facedown on the table. When he picked it up and turned it over, emotion welled in his throat. Inscribed on the mat in big, colorful letters were the words, ''Megan's Daddy.'' The frame held not one picture, but a dozen, a collage showing Ryan, either alone or with Marc, Gabe and Cat. But the one picture that touched him most was in the center, a snapshot of Ryan with his arm around Cat and both of them smiling happily at the camera. Someone— Cat, he was certain—had taken Megan's photo from another picture, trimmed around her and inserted her between her mother and father, just like a family.

''I want Megan always to remember she had a father who would have loved her.''

He glanced up to find Cat in the doorway, sewing kit in hand, watching him. With a nonchalance that hid his feelings, he stood the picture on the table beside the bed.

''Megan's lucky to have a mother like you.'' Glad the bomb's damage to his vocal cords made his voice husky, he took the sewing kit from her hand.

''No, I'm lucky to have Megan,'' Cat insisted.

''Even though you have to raise her alone?''

''Dad makes a terrific grandpa, so I'm not completely alone.''

Silently cursing the circumstances that kept him from claiming his daughter and the woman who should be his wife, he opened the sewing kit and selected a needle and thread.

''Anything missing in here?'' Trace asked as he stitched Pooh's arm back to his body.

Cat shook her head. ''They even left the solid gold locket Dad gave Megan for her last birthday, so either they didn't know it was real gold or they weren't looking for valuables. That's why I think Snake was behind this. He and his buddies did this just for spite.''

Cat had him almost convinced. Ironically, a senseless prank by Snake Larson made the most sense. Once the sheriff had caught the bully and his pals, this ordeal for the Ericksons would be over.

Trace had finished the last stitch on the stuffed animal and knotted the thread when the ring of a telephone sounded through the house.

Cat went into her bedroom to answer it. A few minutes later, she returned, her expression a combination of puzzlement and worry.

''Anything wrong?'' Trace asked.

''That was the sheriff. Last night at nine o'clock, Snake Larson and his buddies were arrested for drunk and disorderly conduct in Bonner's Ferry. They spent the night in jail.''

''Then they couldn't have trashed your house.'' Cold dread settled in Trace's stomach like a poorly digested meal.

Cat's questioning gaze met his. ''If Snake didn't do this, who did?''

Chapter Nine

"The sheriff's certain about the time?" Trace settled his face into a neutral expression, but not before Cat glimpsed the apprehension that had scudded across his features like a fast-moving cloud.

"Positive," Cat said. "He said there's no way Snake and his friends could have been here unless they had wings. And he added they were the least likely candidates for wings he's ever met."

Even her attempt at humor didn't lighten Trace's serious demeanor, and his gravity frightened her. "Why are you so worried?"

"I don't like being in the dark."

She shrugged. "The damage is done, and the culprits are gone now."

He nodded, but his eyes looked past her, as if his grim thoughts were elsewhere. He was a study in contradictions, this tall, muscular man sitting on Megan's frilly bed and holding her Pooh Bear gently in his big hands. Trace had been an exemplary guest, congenial and thoughtful, but Cat guessed he could also be a powerful and dangerous adversary if crossed.

A new and disturbing possibility struck her, almost taking her breath away. "If they weren't after valuables, maybe they were after you."

Trace snapped his attention to her, muscles tensed, hazel eyes veiled. "What makes you say that?"

"You're in military intelligence. You could have made enemies in your line of work. Maybe somebody decided it's payback time."

To her surprise, a slow, amiable grin spread across the handsome contours of his face, dismissing her fears and kicking in a soft flutter just beneath her breastbone. "If they were after me, they could have grabbed me anytime. I was practically alone in town before the graduation. That would have been a perfect time to catch me—if I'm what they wanted."

She lifted her hands in frustration. "So we're back to square one. Who broke in and why?"

"There's always the troublemaking drifters theory."

"Then why didn't they take anything? And don't tell me we scared them off. They could have grabbed Dad's wallet in a heartbeat."

"They did take something."

This time, it was her head that jerked upward in surprise. "What?"

"I don't know."

She scowled in confusion. "Then how do you know something was taken?"

Trace placed Pooh on Megan's pillow and shoved to his feet. "I heard one of them yell from upstairs that he'd found something. As soon as he said it, they left, as if they had what they'd come for.''

"That's a big help," she grumbled.

"It could be," he insisted. "If we can find what's missing, we might be able to figure out why they were here."

"You're certain whatever they took, they found upstairs?" She couldn't think of a thing in the five bedrooms and three baths worth turning a house upside down for.

He placed his hands on her shoulders and gazed at her. The changeable color of his eyes had shifted from a leafy green to smoky brown. "Not certain, but that's how it sounded. We might as well search as we go along, since we have to clean up the rest of the mess anyway."

His eyes sparked with a mesmerizing glint, his breath warmed her cheek, and through the fabric of her blouse, her skin heated at his touch. She found herself remembering every vivid detail of the too-short kiss they'd shared yesterday on the porch. It would be so easy to slide her arms around his neck, stand on tiptoe—

And do something stupid.

Why would kissing him be stupid? she argued with herself. *As long as I remember his presence in my life is only temporary, why can't I enjoy a little dalliance? I've worked hard. I'm entitled to some fun.*

Because you're a commitment kind of gal, her conscience argued back. *You'll think you're engaging in*

*a harmless flirtation, and wham! You'll find yourself
in love. And heartbroken when he leaves for good.*

"Cat?" Trace interrupted her inner debate with a
tiny shake of her shoulders. "You okay? You looked
like you zoned out for a minute."

She could feel the flush ascending to her cheeks,
and she grappled for an explanation. "I was just
thinking which clothes to take to Megan later this
morning. If you'll start in my room, I'll gather her
things and then come help."

He released her, picked up the cleaning supplies
and moved to the next room.

Although he was only a room away, his absence
left her feeling deprived and filled with an overwhelming yearning. Weak-kneed, she sank to Megan's bed and stared at herself in her daughter's
dresser mirror. She had to be losing her mind. How
else could she explain that she was falling in love
with a man she'd known only a few days?

As THE MORNING passed, Trace's frustration doubled.
They'd finished cleaning every room but his, and Cat
couldn't identify a single item that was missing. Adding to his tension was the fact that with him and Cat
alone in the house, he was acutely aware of every
move she made, every word she spoke, every whisper
of her scent that survived above the heavy smell of
cleaning solutions. Her proximity was enough to drive
him dizzy with desire.

Keeping his hands to himself was torture when he
longed to hold her, and he'd almost given in to his

yearning earlier while they were attacking the chaos in her room.

The intruders had flung clothes from her closet and drawers, and Cat had begun gathering them up. She hung skirts and dresses and tossed her very feminine underwear on the bed. When she began creating stacks of the bits of filmy lace and scraps of silk, the sight of her amidst those intimate garments almost made him lose his resistance to lowering her to the bed and making slow, indolent love to her. He managed to control himself, knowing if he tried, she'd think he'd lost his mind and order him to leave.

"What are you doing?" he asked as she continued to sort bras and panties. He found his mouth dry with desire.

"Counting."

"Why?" He hoped she hadn't developed some bizarre obsessive-compulsive disorder centering on undergarments during his long absence.

She turned to face him, hands on her hips, head cocked alluringly to one side. "You said we have to determine what's missing, right?"

He cocked an eyebrow in bewilderment. "You suspect they stole your underwear?"

"No, but if none's taken, we can rule out some weird fetish as a reason for the break-in." She returned to her counting. "Everything's here," she announced and replaced the garments in her bureau.

Disappointment surged through him. Better some testosterone-charged weirdos had invaded the house than fanatical terrorists, he thought, wishing he could find what was taken so he'd know for sure.

He and Cat had moved to Marc's and Gabe's rooms, leaving Trace's room for last.

"Looks like you've already cleaned up in here," she observed from the guest room doorway.

At the sight of her golden-blond curls tied back from her delicately sculpted face with a scarf, intelligent blue eyes that had taken in the room's condition with a glance and delectable curves that neither the plaid shirt nor faded jeans could hide, he took a deep breath and struggled to regain his equilibrium. "I straightened up some before I went down for breakfast, but the bathroom's still a mess. Someone upended a bottle of bath salts in there."

She crossed the room and entered the adjoining bathroom. "Whew! Smells like a brothel in here."

"Really?" he teased. "How would you know?"

She wrinkled her nose in a fetching grimace, and he noted with heart-stopping clarity the faintest trace of freckles scattered across her cheeks, an endearing remnant of the teenager he used to call the Pest.

"Because," she announced in a choking voice, "the stench is cheap, tawdry and overdone."

"At the risk of sounding rude—if you feel that way about those bath salts, why were they here?"

She grinned. "You men don't get it, do you? Why else? Their color matched the tile. I never expected anyone to actually use them."

He joined her in the small room and wielded the broom to sweep the crystals on the floor into a pile while she cleaned the vanity. With the odorous salts captured in a dustpan, he approached the toilet to dump them.

"Don't," Cat warned.

"Why not?"

"They're the foaming kind. I don't know what they'd do to the plumbing or the septic tank."

With a shrug, he dumped the offensive crystals into the wastebasket.

Cat was studying something on the now-clean vanity. "What's this?"

"My shaving kit."

"I've never seen one like it."

"Prince Asim gave it to me. It's crocodile skin."

"Do you mind if I open it? I've been trying to think of what to give Dad for his birthday, and something like this might be just the thing."

The home invaders had emptied the kit, but he'd reassembled it that morning after he shaved.

"Here, I'll open it for you." He grabbed the kit, unzipped it, and with his back to her discreetly palmed the condoms the prince had so generously provided.

"This would be perfect," Cat said. "It has everything. A place for your razor, brush, comb, toothbrush, nail clippers. What goes here?" She pointed to the pocket where the condoms had been.

"Band-Aids," he improvised, slipping the condoms into the pocket of his jeans, "for when I cut myself shaving. But I've used them all up."

"What fits inside this flap with the leather strap across it?"

"A stainless steel mirror."

But the mirror was gone.

"It was there yesterday." Trace glanced around the bathroom but saw no sign of the mirror. "I must have missed it when I was cleaning up."

He went into the bedroom to search, getting on his hands and knees to look under the furniture, but he couldn't find the mirror. Irritated at losing what had been a handy item, he intensified his hunt. Cat joined him.

After they'd turned the guest room upside down, they finally admitted defeat.

"Looks like we found what's missing," Cat said.

"You think they took the mirror? What would they want with a piece of smudged stainless steel—"

Smudges.

Fingerprints.

If someone wanted to verify Trace Gallagher's identity, the mirror would be the perfect tool. Trace needed to talk to Wentworth immediately, but he didn't dare use the Ericksons' phone. If the terrorists had broken in, they could easily have tapped the line.

"The mirror's no great loss." Not wanting to alarm Cat, he shrugged and attempted to appear indifferent. "I could have remembered wrong. Maybe I misplaced it somewhere along the way on my trip from Tabari." Before she could raise further questions, he changed the subject. "Can I ride along when you take

Megan her clothes? I'd like to see the MacIntosh dairy.''

''Sure. Her bag's all packed. If we go now, we can be back here for a late lunch, then tackle the downstairs rooms.''

Cat left to get Megan's things, and Trace made one last desperate search for the mirror.

It was nowhere to be found.

LESS THAN THIRTY minutes later, Trace and Cat arrived at the MacIntosh place, a rambling two-story Victorian farmhouse set on a hill and shaded by tall trees. A huge red barn, a long white dairy barn and other outbuildings sprawled behind it. Unable to admit he'd been there many times before with both Cat and Marc, Trace made the appropriate comments of a first-time visitor. As they approached, he listened attentively to Cat's explanation of the workings of the dairy.

No sooner had they stepped from the SUV than Megan, followed by another pint-size female, raced to meet them. His throat tightened at the sight of his daughter, a perfect amalgam of him and Cat, barreling down the path. She launched herself against his legs and threw her arms around his knees, almost upsetting him in her enthusiasm.

''Trace, come see the kittens. You, too, Mommy.''

''Remember your manners,'' Cat warned. ''Introduce Trace to Jessica.''

The other little girl, a negative image of Megan

with her dark eyes and hair, hung back shyly, twisting a stray curl around her index finger.

"Hello, Jessica. I'm Trace."

"Hi." It was the barest whisper.

"Hey, Jessica," Cat said. "Why don't you and Megan wait for us in the barn? We'll be out to see the kittens after I've spoken with your grandmother."

With obvious relief, the little girl took off toward the back yard with Megan on her heels. Their giggles floated to Trace on the breeze, and he wished the world were as carefree and innocent as those little ones made it seem.

After taking Megan's overnight bag and Pooh Bear from the car, he followed Cat up the walk to the front porch.

Mrs. Mac met them at the screen door and held it open for them to enter. "Have they caught that bunch that caused your trouble?"

"No such luck," Cat said with a shake of her head.

"And how's your father?"

"I spoke with the doctor this morning," Cat said. "He had a broken arm and mild concussion. She wants to keep him a while, but just for observation. His blood pressure's acting up."

Trace spotted a telephone on the hall table. "That reminds me, I have a call to make. May I use your phone?"

"Of course," the older woman said with a warm smile. "Come on back to the kitchen when you've finished. I've made fresh coffee, and the sticky buns are just out of the oven."

The women moved down the hall. Trace picked up the phone and punched in Wentworth's number.

"I think we have a problem," Trace said as soon as the colonel answered. He quickly described the break-in at the ranch and his missing mirror. "I may be way off base, but I don't want to take any chances. Can you have my prints pulled from the national database, or at least have the FBI change them to Gallagher's name?"

"I'll see what I can do and let you know."

"Don't call the ranch." Trace rattled off the MacIntoshes' number. "The neighbors can bring me a message if you need to get in touch with me."

"No memories yet?"

"Sorry, sir."

"Now would be a good time."

"No one wants to remember as much as I do. I have a daughter I didn't know about. If the terrorists discover me, her life's at stake, as well as Cat and Gabe Erickson's."

"Understood. I'll be in touch."

Frustrated that he could do no more, Trace returned the receiver to its cradle and joined Mrs. Mac and Cat in the sunny kitchen where the mouthwatering smell of fresh baked goods mingled with the smell of coffee.

Cat gave him a curious glance. "Did you make your call?"

"Yes, to an old Marine buddy in San Francisco," Trace lied. "He's expecting me for a visit, and I told him I'll be staying here a while. I reversed the charges, Mrs. Mac.''

"That was thoughtful, dear, but unnecessary." She placed a plate with a sticky bun the size of a saucer in front of him. "I have one of those pennies-a-minute rates. Have to, to keep in touch with the family, because my daughters are flung out over four states.''

Trace accepted a cup of coffee with thanks and attacked the sticky bun. If he was lucky, Wentworth would call back before he and Cat left. The sooner Trace learned whether his identity was safe the better. For all of them.

AT THE RANCH much later that afternoon while replacing books on the living room shelves, Cat studied Trace from the corner of her eye. He was using wood glue and C-clamps to repair the leg of an end table broken by the intruders, and she found herself fascinated by the deft, graceful movements of his long, slender hands.

Earlier, those same hands had handled the reins skillfully when he'd helped her exercise the horses after their return from the MacIntosh farm. His powerful thighs had gripped his mount with experienced ease, and even Rogue, the most unruly horse in the stable, had continued to respond with surprising cooperation to Trace's firm but gentle touch.

The man was a contradiction of strength and tenderness. At the dairy, he had sat cross-legged in the hay with Megan and Jessica and played with the five-week-old kittens. The little balls of fur had been dwarfed by his big hands, and he hadn't protested when they dug their sharp claws into his shirt and jeans and crawled all over him. If anything, he'd appeared to be having the time of his life. For almost an hour, he and the girls had laughed at the kittens' antics and discussed with fitting seriousness appropriate names for the petite felines.

Observing his gentleness with the animals and his playfulness with the children had been enough to melt any woman's heart. As a result, Cat found herself more vulnerable than ever to the considerable charm of their houseguest.

"You're good with children," she told him on the drive home.

"Prince Asim had eight youngsters, all under twelve. My duties often included guarding them, so I've had a lot of experience."

"It's more than experience. I've known teachers who've spent their whole lives around kids, but they're still stiff and uncomfortable with them. You're a natural."

"From what I observed at graduation, you have a knack with young people yourself."

"Relating to my students comes easier to me since Megan was born."

"You're a terrific mother."

The unmistakably warm approval in his eyes had pleased her. "Megan's a terrific kid. There isn't anything I wouldn't do for my little girl."

"She doesn't seem spoiled."

"I don't mean I pamper her. I see too many of my students whose parents feel they can substitute material things and excessive freedom for what they fail to give their kids."

"Like love?"

"Love, self-confidence, goals, discipline. Parenting done right, Dad always tells me, is the hardest—and most rewarding—job on earth. What makes me sad is knowing what a fantastic father Ryan would have been. He and Megan both are missing out on a lot."

"I'm sure Ryan knows what a great job you're doing with his daughter." Trace's voice had caressed her, softening the pain in her heart at Ryan's absence.

The man was amazing, always choosing the right words or actions in any situation. Only one matter in the entire idyllic afternoon had seemed off-key. In the dairy barn, Trace had glanced constantly toward the house, as if expecting someone. And once they'd returned to High Valley, he often cocked his head to listen or gazed out the window as if hoping to see a vehicle approach.

While she watched surreptitiously from the bookcase, he turned his head again, as if anticipating an arrival.

"Are you expecting someone?" she asked.

He glanced up from the table he was repairing. An unreadable expression skipped across his face before his features settled into a smile. "It would be just like Gabe to check himself out of the hospital, commandeer a ride home and surprise us."

"He'd have to sneak past the doctor. I called her

while you were rubbing down Rogue. She wants to keep him until tomorrow morning.''

Trace frowned in concern. ''His blood pressure still up?''

''It's normal. She just wants to make sure it stays that way.'' A sudden thought filled Cat with dread. ''You don't think the men who did this will come back?''

He shook his head. ''Why should they? If they're thieves, they would have taken what they wanted last night.''

''And if they're not?''

''Then they're vandals who'll get their kicks from trashing someone else's place next time.''

''Then why did they take your mirror?''

''We don't know that they did. I might have lost it earlier.''

Again, Trace's voice and words consoled her. His presence reassured her. With his finely tuned muscles and well-trained strength, he stood like a bulwark between her and danger.

But, a small inner voice said, *why do you get the feeling he's not telling you something?*

She shook away the disturbing thought. The invasion and wreckage of her home had made her paranoid.

Noting a drapery yanked from its hooks, she replaced the last book on the shelf and headed for the utility closet in the kitchen to retrieve the stepladder. She found it jammed in the back of the space behind the vacuum cleaner and attempted to tug it free.

"Let me get that," Trace said behind her.

She turned in the close confines of the closet to find her nose pressed almost to his chest. Mixed with the lemony aroma of furniture polish, the warm, musky scent of him shot pangs of longing through her. With difficulty, she resisted the temptation to twine her arms around his waist and rest her head against his heart. Her own was beating a tattoo as fierce as a Blackfoot war drum's.

She managed to catch her breath enough to mumble thanks, then wiggled past him out the door.

What was wrong with her?

True, she hadn't made love to a man since Ryan, because she'd never believed in sex simply for sex's sake. But she didn't want sex. She wanted to make love to Trace. But how could she allow herself to fall in love with someone when she knew he'd leave soon? She didn't want to mourn the loss of another man.

Shaken by the intensity of her longing, she retreated to the living room on wobbly legs. By the time Trace appeared with the ladder, her breathing had slowed almost to normal, and only her telltale blush betrayed her lack of composure.

"Where do you want this?" He hefted the ladder easily in one hand.

She pointed to the tall window beside the fireplace, and Trace unfolded the ladder and secured the braces.

"Want me to fix that?" He pointed to the drapery that had been pulled loose from the traverse rod.

"I'll get it." Cat scrambled to the top of the ladder,

glad for an excuse to focus on anything except the hypnotic appeal of the man behind her.

"Be care—"

Before he could complete his warning, Cat felt her boot slip on the rung. She leaned sideways to grab the stones of the fireplace for balance, but her jerky movement only hastened her fall. As if in slow motion, she pitched off the ladder into space.

And landed in Trace's arms.

Instinctively, she threw her arms around his neck. He tightened his grip, drawing her along the rock-solid length of him as she slid to her feet. But she didn't let go. Overpowered by an all-consuming feeling of coming home, she remained in his arms, her head tilted, her gaze locked with his.

Desire glistened in his eyes and pulsed in the vein at his neck, and his words surprised her, contradicting the hunger in his expression. "We can't do this."

"You're absolutely right," she agreed, unable to tear her eyes from his or her arms from around his neck.

"We barely know one another." He continued to hold her close without the slightest loosening of his embrace.

"It's been only a few days," she acknowledged.

"And I'll be leaving soon."

"That's true."

The idea of his walking out of her life as quickly as he'd entered jolted her anew.

With stunning clarity, she recognized why she loved this man. She admired his compassion, his gentleness, his care for her family, his strength in a crisis. She loved his companionship, his conversation, his sense of humor. What she felt for Trace wasn't mere lust, but genuine caring. And, like Ryan, he soon would walk out of her life and be gone forever.

The prospect made her crazy.

Standing on tiptoe, she lifted her face closer to his. His breath brushed her cheek, sending delicious shivers down her spine.

"We have no future together," he argued, his deep voice huskier than usual.

"You're right." She was having trouble breathing and could hardly speak. Her mouth was saying one thing, but her heart was denying every word.

"We can't afford to get involved." The look in his eyes made a liar of him.

"Right again. It wouldn't be fair to either of us," she agreed.

She placed her hands on his chest to push away but found herself instead twining her fingers in his shirt, reveling in the heat of him and drawing him closer. His lips claimed hers, and an irrepressible moan escaped her throat. He crushed her to him, and along the length of contact her body burned like a white-hot flame.

Breaking off their kiss, he lifted her in his arms, carried her to the sofa and settled her on his lap. His hands kneaded the muscles of her back, and he trailed kisses down the length of her throat to the sensitive skin at the opening of her blouse. Arching against him, she yielded to the exquisite torture of his touch.

With a hoarse cry, he broke away. "We can't do this," he repeated.

Shaken and wanting him as badly as she'd ever wanted Ryan, she searched his face for a hint of rejection. All she found was stark need mixed with tenderness, his expression a mirror of her desire.

"Why not?"

He gasped for air like a drowning man going under for the third time. "For all the reasons we've already mentioned."

He was right, but her heart had left reason behind in the dust. "None of them are insurmountable."

Panic flickered through his hazel eyes before his expression calmed and cleared. "As much as I want to make love to you, I can't, not without protection."

If she hadn't witnessed his need and felt his response to her, she would have believed that he didn't want her, but she knew better. Decent and unselfish, Trace was trying to do the right thing.

The problem was, Cat didn't want the right thing. She wanted him.

With a defiant toss of her head, she fixed him with a seductive smile. "We can always use the condoms you slipped in your pocket this morning."

He blinked in surprise. "You saw me?"

She shrugged and allowed herself a self-satisfied smirk. "Your back was to me, but you were standing in front of a mirror."

His grin outclassed hers. "Why, you sneaky little—"

She stopped his accusation with her lips.

AN HOUR LATER, Trace sat on the sofa with Cat curled asleep against his bare chest. He tugged the Navajo blanket closer around her, covering her naked shoulders, and stroked her thick, fine hair.

He'd been a damned fool.

Not that he regretted making love to Cat. When she'd shed her clothes and they'd come together in a flurry of passion and need, he'd feared he would die of happiness. Ever since his memory had returned, he'd dreamed of being with her again. When their bodies had joined, what they'd shared had been even more magnificent than he'd remembered.

Like two pieces of the same being once broken apart, they had merged into one perfect whole. The first time, their lovemaking had been frantic with need born of years of loneliness and separation, a turbulent coupling that left them gasping for air, shaken by the intensity of the experience.

The second time, Trace had loved her with a slow, languorous reverence. When they both were sated, he had clamped his lips to hold back the words, ''I love you.''

Not knowing what the future held, he couldn't commit to her, couldn't lead her to expect him to stay—or even to return once he'd gone away. Worst of all, he worried what she'd think if the time did come when he could reveal his identity. Would she hate him for misleading her, for making love to her under false pretenses? And had she come to care enough for Trace Gallagher that his leaving would break her heart?

Again.

A damned fool is right. His conscience denounced him.

Cat stirred in his arms, and the sensation of her bare skin against his would have aroused him to make love to her again if he hadn't been so worried.

A glance at the antique clock on the mantel indicated almost five o'clock, hours since he'd contacted Wentworth about the fingerprints. The more time that passed without Wentworth's reassurance that Ryan's prints had been safeguarded, the more worried he grew.

What the hell was taking Wentworth so long?

As if in answer to his question, the hum of an approaching engine and the crunch of tires on gravel sounded on the road to the ranch.

With a gentle shake, he awakened Cat. ''Someone's coming. You'd better get dressed.''

''I'll be right back.'' With a slow smile and a quick kiss, she picked up her clothes and scooted upstairs.

Trace quickly pulled on his jeans, shirt and boots, and was standing at the front door when Mrs. Mac's oldest son, George, stepped onto the porch.

''I have a message for you from somebody named Wentworth. I would have called you, but he insisted I deliver it in person.'' He handed Trace a paper. ''Wrote it down to make sure I got it right.''

''Thanks—''

''Can't stay. Have to get back for the evening milking.''

George trotted to his truck, and Trace watched him

go. The paper burned in his hand, but he waited until the vehicle disappeared down the road before he unfolded and read it.

Wentworth's message was as bad as it could get.

Chapter Ten

Trace scanned the message from Wentworth again, hoping he'd misread it the first time.

He hadn't.

"Unknown hacker accessed files before prints pulled," the colonel had reported. "Cover blown. Take family immediately to safe house at base in Great Falls and wait for further orders."

"Something wrong?" Cat stood on the stairs, her cheeks still pink from lovemaking and sleep.

Trace experienced a sinking feeling in the pit of his stomach. In spite of his careful charade—or because of it—he'd landed the woman he loved, her father and his daughter in terrible jeopardy.

"About as wrong as it can get," he admitted.

"What is it?"

"You'd better sit down. There's something I have to tell you."

Dammit, he'd wanted all along to reveal who he really was, to come clean with her, but not this way. Not with killers on their trail who gave him no time to explain properly. No time to lessen the shock or soften the blow.

Her knees seemed to give way, and she grabbed the banister for support. "Megan? Daddy?"

"They're fine, but you're all in danger."

He took her by the arm, led her to the sofa and eased her onto the cushions. Her brow wrinkled, and she sat staring at him with puzzled eyes.

"I've just learned the men who broke in last night weren't vandals," he said. "They're terrorists, part of a group called Righteous Sword."

"The same ones who bombed the embassy?" Confusion darkened her irises to midnight blue. "What would terrorists want with us?"

"Not you or Gabe. They were looking for me."

"I don't understand."

"They were trying to find out my real identity. That's why they took the mirror from my shaving kit. It had my fingerprints. George MacIntosh just brought a message from my commanding officer. A hacker has broken into AFIS—"

"Aphis?"

"The FBI's automated fingerprint identification system. The terrorists know now who I really am."

She shook her head in befuddlement. "You're not Trace Gallagher?"

"No." Dear God, would she despise him for his deception? And would she give him time to explain five lost years?

"Then who are you?"

He took a deep breath. Everything was riding on

his next words, but how could he even begin to explain?

"*Kalila—*"

Her eyes widened with shock, her hand flew to her mouth, and the color drained from her face. "No, you can't be—"

He knelt before her and grasped her shoulders. "I'm Ryan, Cat. I've wanted to tell you—"

Her expression crinkled with disbelief. "If you're Ryan, why don't you look like Ryan?"

"They had to rebuild most of me after the bombing."

She searched his face, measured his features and stared deep into his eyes. Her summery blue ones lit with sudden recognition. And joy. "Oh, God, I can't believe it's true. You're really alive."

"I wanted to tell you before—"

She threw her arms around him and buried her head on his shoulder. Her body shook with sobs.

"Don't cry, please."

"I can't help it. I'm so happy." As if the thought had just struck her, she cocked her head and glared at him through her tears. "Where have you been all these years?"

With reluctance, he untwined her arms from his neck and pushed her gently away. "I'll tell you everything you want to know later."

"But—"

"Right now you must pack for you, Megan and Gabe. I have to take you all to safety at the base in Great Falls before the terrorists come looking for us."

"I thought you said they didn't want us, just you."

"Now that they know I'm Ryan, they're after me and everyone close to me."

She shook her head in confusion. "Why?"

"To find out what I know and who I told. Then to kill all of us—"

"Kill us?"

"They're desperate to eliminate anyone who can identify them."

The mixture of hurt, fear, confusion and happiness in her eyes tore at him, but he didn't have time for more explanations.

"Hurry and pack. Take the minimum, because we have to get moving. We'll pick up Megan and Gabe on the way out."

She touched his face with her fingers, a light, feathery contact as gentle as a kiss, then pushed past him to run up the stairs.

HER NAME—Ryan's pet name for her—on his lips had convinced her.

Kalila.

For five long years she had longed to hear Ryan call her that just one more time.

But his distinctive khaki-colored eyes had been the key. Looking back, she realized her subconscious had recognized him by his unusual greenish-brown eyes that first day he'd appeared in her classroom.

No wonder she'd felt so drawn to him. She hadn't fallen in love with a stranger. Her heart had recognized Ryan.

Stumbling up the stairs in her haste, she attempted to sort through a jumble of emotions.

Joy.

Anger.

Hurt.

If he'd kept his existence secret for all this time, could she trust him now?

She hurried into Megan's room, and concern for her daughter's safety ended her hesitation. If the slightest chance existed that Megan could be harmed, Cat wasn't about to take it. She'd seen Ryan with her daughter—their daughter—and although she wasn't sure of anything else at this point, she was certain he would never do anything to hurt Megan.

Rushing from room to room, Cat gathered the barest necessities for herself, her dad and Megan and stuffed them in a backpack. She met Ryan at the top of the stairs. He had his duffel bag slung across his shoulder.

"Ready?" he asked in that strange, husky voice that must have been caused by bomb damage.

Unable to trust her own voice, she nodded, then followed him down the stairs and out the door to the car.

Once he'd stowed their bags in the back, he held out his hand. "You'd better let me drive. Things could get hairy if we meet these guys on the road."

She tossed him the keys and climbed into the passenger seat. Ryan slid behind the wheel, started the engine and took off in a flurry of gravel and dust.

Since learning he was Ryan, one detail had nagged

at her, and Cat could contain her hurt no longer. "Why didn't you tell me you'd survived?"

"Because I didn't know myself until three weeks ago." He kept his eyes on the road and his white-knuckled grip on the wheel. A muscle ticked with tension at the base of his square jaw.

Cat felt as if she were trapped in a surreal dream and couldn't wake up. For almost three days, he'd lived in her house, claiming to be Trace Gallagher. Little more than an hour earlier, he'd made love to her with both ferocity and tenderness.

Now he'd told her that he was really Ryan, and they were all in danger. But when she demanded explanations, his answers made no sense.

He reached for her hand and squeezed it gently. "Trust me, Cat. I didn't desert you. I suffered amnesia after the blast. Between the military and Asim, they convinced me I was Trace Gallagher, one of Asim's bodyguards. Everything I told you about living in the prince's household was true."

She wanted to believe him, but she still ached too much from his deception to be completely trusting.

She shook her head, knowing she should withdraw her hand but unable to resist the comfort of his touch. "Why did the Marines tell us you were dead?"

"For your protection—and mine."

"I don't understand." The words came out with a sob. Her skin flushed hot, then cold, and she wondered if she was going into shock.

"Right before Marc went into a coma," Ryan explained, "he told the men who found him that I could identify the traitor in the embassy, the man who was working with the terrorists. Before the brass could put a lid on that info, it had spread among the survivors. If the terrorists had known I was alive and if I had contacted you, they would have killed us both.''

''I would have kept your secrets.'' His lack of trust stung her.

''I know, but it wasn't up to me.'' He squeezed her hand again. ''The first thing I tried to do when my memory returned was to call you. But Asim's bodyguards hustled me straight to Colonel Barker. He sent me directly to the counterterrorist unit at the Pentagon. I wasn't allowed any phone calls. Once I realized how much danger you'd be in, as much as I wanted to see you or just to hear your voice, I didn't dare put you at risk by letting you know I was alive.''

As he drove, taking the mountain curves at maximum speed, he told her how Wentworth had hoped coming to Montana would cure his amnesia.

''But you still can't remember those days before the bombing?'' she asked.

He shook his head. ''When I learned Marc had said nothing to you that would identify the traitors, I called Wentworth to report. I wanted to leave.''

''Why?'' Her heart sank. Had she misread his affection? Had his caring for her and their unforgettable lovemaking been part of his pretense?

The glance he threw her was filled with agony and despair. ''Being close to you and Megan, not being able to tell you the truth, not being able to touch you, to hold you, was sheer torture. I couldn't risk leading the terrorists to you if I confessed my real identity. Even staying as Trace Gallagher would be too risky.''

"Then why didn't you leave?" Her head spun, trying to absorb all that he told her.

"Wentworth ordered me to stay. I might have disobeyed those orders, but when Gabe was hurt, I remained here to help out. You know the rest.''

A puzzle nagged at her. "How did the terrorists locate you so quickly?"

"They probably still have contacts in the embassy. Possibly even in Asim's palace. When I was jerked out of Tabari so quickly and sent to the Pentagon, then ended up in Ryan Christopher's and Marc Erickson's old stomping grounds, the circumstances must have made them nervous. They had to find out who I really was.''

"And now they know you're Ryan.''

He nodded, his face grim. "I'm the one man still alive who can ID who's connected to the embassy bombing.'' He slammed the wheel with his fist. "If I could only remember.''

After his outburst, he grew quiet and concentrated on the treacherous hairpin curves. She took the opportunity to study his profile. In her classroom the day of his arrival, she'd been positive at first glance that he was Ryan, but then the subtle changes in his appearance had thrown her. Now, reading the firm line of his jaw, the patrician shape of his nose—minus the bump from his childhood brawl, the familiar arch of his brow and the jut of his chin, she could see the Ryan she remembered had been there all along.

Her heart ached for the injuries he'd sustained. The fact that his nose had been straightened, his cheekbones lifted and the cleft in his chin erased testified to the extensive surgeries he'd undergone. He must have suffered untold physical agonies. Add to that the psychological distress of amnesia, and his very existence must have been pure hell after the bombing. And he'd had no friends, no family to help him through those tough times. He must have felt again like that lost and lonely little boy who'd been abandoned at a Chicago church.

She wondered how emotionally scarred his experiences had left him. With a flush of heat, she remembered from their lovemaking the multitude of physical scars, evidence of the damage his body had endured.

How could she not have recognized him? She'd missed so many clues. Rogue had accepted the so-called stranger. How could a horse recognize its former owner when she hadn't identified the man she loved?

And the fingerprints. She understood now why Trace had argued against the crime techs dusting the house. They would have uncovered his secret.

And the love in his eyes when he looked at Megan. No wonder the poor man was so smitten. Megan was his very own daughter.

In retrospect, Cat felt a perfect idiot for not knowing. If nothing else, her immediate strong feelings for him should have tipped her off. But none of that mattered now. All that mattered was that Ryan was alive and he loved her.

And she loved him.

"I'm glad you're home," Cat said, putting all the warmth and sincerity she could muster into her tone. "Your family's missed you."

"I didn't want to make love to you until I could tell you the truth," he said, as if reading her thoughts.

"I think I've sensed that you were Ryan all along," she admitted. "Why else could I have fallen in love with a total stranger?"

He reached across and brushed a curl off her cheek. "I've caused you too much pain. First thinking I'm dead. Now running for our lives. You deserve better, *Kalila.*"

She grasped his hand and planted a kiss on his palm. "How could I have better when I already have the best?"

He pulled his hand to the steering wheel and seemed to withdraw into himself. "There's no future with me, Cat. Not as long as those killers are after me."

"Then you and your Colonel Wentworth will just have to catch them," she said with fierce intensity, "because I'm not losing you again, Ryan Christopher. And Megan's not giving up her father."

Her words were laced with bravado, but fear filled her heart as they turned onto the road that led to the MacIntosh dairy. They had yet to pick up Megan and Gabe, and they were still a long way from Great Falls and safety.

"As far as everyone else is concerned," Ryan said as they approached the house, "I'm still Trace Gallagher."

"Everyone except Dad," Cat said.

Ryan nodded. "We'll tell him once we've left the hospital.

If we make it that far.

"What about telling Megan?" he asked

"She's going to be very confused. We'd better wait until we can explain things a little bit at a time."

Ryan checked the rearview mirror to make sure no one was following. Getting away from the ranch and out of Athens was taking too much time, and as long as they remained in the area, they were an easy target for the terrorists.

He ducked his head to scan the sky through the windshield. Cloud cover obscured the mountaintops. The weather conditions nixed the possibility of requesting Wentworth to lift them out by chopper. They'd have to take the roads.

And their chances.

He stopped the car in front of the house. "We have to get in and out of here fast."

Cat nodded and hopped from the SUV. Ryan followed her to the door where Mrs. Mac stood waiting.

"I heard your car on the drive. Is everything all right?" Curiosity and concern burned in the older woman's eyes.

Ryan knew someone in the household had taken Wentworth's message and probably shared its contents with the others, but for the safety of their good neighbors, he didn't dare elaborate on his situation.

"We've come for Megan," Cat said. "We're going

out of town for a few days. A family emergency."

"I put her to bed," Mrs. Mac said, "less than thirty minutes ago."

"No need to wake her," Ryan said easily, tamping down his impatience. He'd never felt more like a sitting duck, and he hated that Cat and Megan were targets, too. "I'll carry her to the car, and she can sleep in her booster seat."

Mr. Mac had joined his wife in the entry hall. "Made arrangements for your livestock while you're away?"

Cat blinked in confusion, and Ryan felt a stab of sympathy for her. With all the emotions and information she'd had to assimilate in the past hour, someone to care for the animals at the ranch was probably the last thing on her mind.

"Could your grandsons take charge for a day or two?" Ryan asked. "Just until we can make other arrangements?"

"Don't see why not," the older man agreed. He and his wife exchanged a long look. They obviously knew something wasn't right, but they were too polite to ask.

"Megan's in the last room on the right, just down the hall," Mrs. Mac said.

Feeling the pressure of time running out, Ryan started down the corridor, and Cat followed on his heels.

"You get Megan," she said. "I'll get her things."

He opened the bedroom door, and light from the

hallway illuminated two twin beds. In the first, Jessica slept peacefully, her curls a dark spot against the white linen pillowslip.

The other bed was empty.

Ryan whirled and called to Mrs. Mac. "She's gone."

Mrs. Mac's eyebrows lifted in alarm. "That's not possible. Try the bathroom across the hall."

Ryan opened the door and flicked on the light. The white-tiled room was empty.

"She's not there." Cat's voice verged on panic. "Where is she?"

"Gramma?" Jessica sat up in her bed and rubbed her eyes. "What's going on?"

Mrs. Mac rushed to her granddaughter's side. "We're looking for Megan, sweetie. Do you know where she is?"

Jessica nodded solemnly. "But I promised I wouldn't tell."

Mrs. Mac grasped the girl's shoulders and looked her in the eye. "Promises are important, but Megan's mother needs her. You'll have to break your word this time."

Jessica hesitated, and Ryan stifled the urge to shake the little darling. The clock was ticking down the seconds, each minute decreasing their chance of escaping before the terrorists came for them.

"Megan went to the barn," Jessica finally admitted, "to sleep with the kitties. She said they were lonesome."

Ryan heaved a sigh of relief. "I'll get her. Cat, take her things to the car, and I'll meet you there."

"I'll go with you," Mr. Mac said to him.

The men went through the kitchen, where Mr. Mac stopped to exchange his house slippers for boots. The farm was quiet, with only the gentle lowing of cows from the dairy breaking the stillness as the men crossed the back yard to the horse barn in the gathering gloom. Mr. Mac opened the barn door, slipped through first and turned on the lights.

Ryan went straight to the stall where he'd played with his daughter and the kittens. The tabby and her offspring were there, curled up fast asleep.

There was no sign of Megan.

"You search the barn," Mr. Mac said. "I'll call my boys to help."

The farmer left, and Ryan stood for a moment, hoping to hear a childish giggle above the snuffling of the horses and the plaintive mew of an unhappy kitten.

"Megan," he called. "Come out if you're here. Your mommy's waiting for you. We're going on a trip."

He cocked his head and listened, but only the noises of the animals broke the stillness.

Hoping Megan might be sound asleep somewhere in the building, Ryan raced through the barn, searching every corner and crevice. Outside, the clang of a large bell, muffled only slightly by the fog, echoed off the surrounding mountains. Its clamor would be heard clearly by the MacIntosh sons who lived in their own homes nearby.

Ryan was inspecting the hayloft when the barn door flew open and Cat rushed in.

He hurried down the ladder to meet her.

"Where's Megan?" she demanded.

The terror in her face stabbed through him, filling him with reproach. "We don't know. Mr. Mac's alerting his sons to help us search."

Cat grabbed his arm so tightly her nails dug into his skin. "Megan would never wander off without permission. She knows better."

Ryan refused to allow himself to think the worst. "Maybe one of the kittens got loose, and she went after it. It's not dark yet. We'll find her."

Outside the barn, they found Mr. Mac with his sons George and Greg and three teenage grandsons, who had gathered in the yard in response to the emergency bell. The boys rode all-terrain vehicles.

"We'll search farther out," the oldest grandson said, and the three took off in separate directions.

"I'll check the dairy barn," Mr. Mac said. "George and Greg, check the chicken coop and pigsty. Catherine and Mr. Gallagher can look nearest the house."

The farmer handed them flashlights, and the group broke up to search.

Ryan stayed with Cat. He'd given her the flashlight, but her hand shook so hard, the bobbing light proved useless. His heart beating in his throat with fear for his child, he drew Cat to him and wrapped his arms around her. She was shivering, as much from fright as the chilly night air.

"We'll find her," he said in the most convincing tone he could summon. "She hasn't been out of Mrs. Mac's sight for more than half an hour. With those short little legs, she can't go far."

"Unless someone took her."

"Shh." He stroked her hair, then squeezed her tight. "Don't even think that. We'll find her."

"But she's so little, and the farm's such a big place." She hiccuped, swallowing a sob.

Ryan didn't even want to think about the wild animals that prowled the surrounding forest. "Then we'd better start looking. Give me the light, and you hold on to me."

An hour later, after searching beneath every shrub and tree around the house and the length of the drive to the main road, Ryan discovered his confidence in finding Megan severely shaken.

"Let's get back to the house," he said. "One of the others has probably found her already, and they're all drinking hot chocolate in Mrs. Mac's kitchen."

Although he tried to sound reassuring, his voice rang hollowly in his ears. Cat's exhaustion was evident as she struggled to put one foot in front of the other.

When they reached the front porch, the others were there ahead of them.

"No sign of her anywhere," Mr. Mac announced grimly.

The screen door slammed, and Jessica, barefoot in her nightgown, pulled on Mrs. Mac's sleeve.

"Go back to bed," her grandmother ordered. "You'll catch pneumonia out here in the night air."

"But, Gramma—"

"No buts, young lady. March."

Jessica turned to go back in the house, and Ryan spied the stuffed animal in her hand.

"Wait," he called to her. "What have you got?"

"It's Megan's teddy." The little girl held the bear in front of her. "That's what I was trying to tell Gramma. Somebody sticked him."

Ryan's heart froze at the sight of a folded piece of paper attached to the bear's chest with a safety pin and fluttering in the breeze. Written in bold block letters across the front of the note was a name.

Ryan Christopher.

Chapter Eleven

The nondescript middle-aged man stood in front of the lighted shop window on the New York City street. With his hands clasped behind his back, he appeared to study the specialty cheeses and Italian sausages arrayed behind the glass. Passersby paid him little attention.

When the pay phone on the street corner rang, the man reached it in three quick strides.

"Do you have them?" Derrick Hutton asked after the caller had identified himself.

"Not all of them."

"What do you mean, not all?"

"Christopher, the woman and her father had left the ranch by the time we arrived. We approached on a logging road from the east, hoping to surprise them. They had already left by the main road."

Hutton silently cursed the incompetence of his operatives. "If you didn't get them, who else is there?"

"The little girl."

"Who?"

"Ryan Christopher's four-year-old daughter.

Yacoub grabbed her at the neighbors' while the rest of us hit the ranch.''

"What good is a child?" Hutton's voice dripped with sarcasm. "She can tell us nothing we need to know."

"She is bait for bigger fishes. We will use her to draw the others into our net."

"Just make certain they don't bring the authorities with them," Hutton warned. "You must grab Christopher fast. Once you have him, interrogate him within an inch of his life. Find out what he knows and who he's told."

"It's been five years. If he's a threat, wouldn't he have blown the whistle on you by now?"

"That's what I must determine," Hutton said. "It's possible he knows nothing. It's more likely he's set the FBI and the military on our trail."

"Then why have we not seen them?"

Hutton snorted. "Do you know nothing? They could be waiting to ascertain our plans, to widen their trap."

"And once I've learned everything Christopher has to tell us?"

Hutton didn't hesitate. "Kill them all, the whole cursed family. Let their deaths be a warning to those who would betray us."

Hutton slammed the receiver into its cradle and stomped toward his apartment, his interest in cheese and sausages forgotten.

CAT PUSHED past Ryan and plucked Megan's teddy bear from Jessica's hands. With trembling fingers, she ripped the crudely addressed note from the animal's chest and opened it.

The one-line message was in Arabic.

Her knees would have given way if Ryan hadn't slid his arm around her in support. She handed him the paper.

"What does it say?" Cat asked.

A muscle ticked rapidly in Ryan's tightly clenched jaw. "Nothing. It's just a signature."

"Whose?"

He inhaled a deep breath, as if steadying himself before he spoke. "Righteous Sword."

"Oh, God," Cat moaned. "The terrorists. They have my baby?"

"What's going on?" Mr. Mac demanded. "Has someone kidnapped the girl?"

Despite her overwhelming fear for Megan, Cat knew she had to stay calm. Dissolving into hysterics wouldn't help her daughter. She gazed at the circle of worried MacIntosh faces that surrounded her, not knowing how to explain what had happened. The more she told them, the more danger they faced, but they knew too much already to keep them in the dark. She glanced up at Ryan. "We have to tell them. We'll need all the help we can get to look for her."

Ryan was staring at the teddy bear. "Where did you find this, Jessica?"

"On the back porch."

Cat shook her head in denial and fought to hold herself together, afraid if she stopped to think about her daughter's circumstances, she'd shatter into a million pieces. "It wasn't there earlier when we searched around the house. We would have seen it."

"Let's go inside," Mrs. Mac offered. "We'll settle nothing out here in the cold. I'll fix something hot to drink, and you can tell us what's going on."

"I should call the sheriff first," Mr. Mac said.

"No," Ryan said sharply. "Not yet."

"We have to do *something*," Cat cried. "We can't just let those murderers have Megan."

At her words, George and Greg exchanged glances, then ordered their teenage sons to return home. As soon as the boys had driven away on the ATVs, Mrs. Mac whisked Jessica off to bed, and the adults gathered in the kitchen.

Cat moved like a sleepwalker, unable to comprehend the horror that had struck her. When Ryan pulled out a chair at the table and nudged her into it, she sat without resistance, feeling again the erratic sensations of hot and cold and wondering once more if she was going into shock.

Mr. and Mrs. Mac, George and Greg joined her around the table. Ryan remained standing.

"We didn't want to involve you in this," he said, "but since you know so much already, I'll have to tell the rest. Then, Mr. Mac, you'll understand my reluctance to involve the sheriff."

Without wasting words, Ryan filled them in on his survival of the embassy bombing, his attempt to identify the terrorists and Righteous Sword's subsequent discovery of his true identity. Cat watched him, amazed at his coolness while his daughter was in the hands of terrorists, until she looked into his eyes. The raw pain and guilt reflected there made her look away.

"Surely they won't harm a little girl?" Mrs. Mac said when he'd finished his tale.

"They want to find out what I know about them," Ryan told her, "and then, if they follow the pattern they've used in the past, they will probably kill my entire family as a vendetta."

The kindly woman's elderly face paled. "And *my* family?"

Ryan shook his head. "I honestly don't know. But for your sakes, Cat and I should leave as soon as possible."

The conversation swirled around Cat like a fog, barely penetrating the icy fear that gripped her. The more she tried not to think of her daughter in the hands of strangers, the stronger the picture formed in her mind. Aching to hold Megan and keep her safe, she wrapped her arms around herself in a vain attempt to quell her shaking.

"Where will you go from here?" Mr. Mac was asking Ryan. "And what will you do about Megan?"

"I'm taking Cat into town," Ryan said. "We'll pick up her father there, and I'll ask Todd Brewster to drive them to the safe house."

His intention registered through the fog of fear that enveloped her.

"No!" Cat jumped from her chair. "Todd can take Dad to safety, but I'm not going, not as long as Megan's out there somewhere. I won't turn my back on my daughter.''

Ryan grasped her shoulders, lowered his face close to hers and spoke in a low and pleading tone. ''We don't know what the kidnappers want. That isn't a ransom note.'' He nodded toward the torn and crumpled sheet of paper she still clutched in her hand. ''Maybe they'll exchange Megan for me.''

When she'd thought the pain could be no worse, fresh agony stabbed through her. Ryan had just returned to her. She couldn't bear the thought of losing him again.

''We have to get her back,'' Cat said with unbending resolve. She reached up and placed her hand over his on her shoulder. ''And keep you safe. Can't your Colonel Wentworth help us?''

Mr. Mac, his weathered face grim, stood and spoke to George and Greg. ''You two should go home to your families. George, take Jessica with you. I don't want either of you involved any more in this.''

''What about you and Mom?'' Greg asked, obviously reluctant to abandon his parents.

Mr. Mac shook his head. ''We'll be all right.''

Ryan thanked the MacIntosh sons for their help in the search, but Cat was so dazed she barely noticed when the men left the room.

''Now,'' Mr. Mac said, once his boys were gone, ''what can Myra and I do to help?''

Ryan shook his head. ''I don't want to place you at any more risk. I'm sorry we had to involve you at all.''

Mr. Mac scowled. "I don't hold with terrorists. And I care even less for scoundrels who steal children. If people like us don't stand up against 'em, who will?"

"He's right," Mrs. Mac agreed with an emphatic nod. "Just tell us what to do."

"We must make sure Gabriel's safe," Ryan said.

"But we can't tell him Megan's been kidnapped," Cat added quickly. "His blood pressure can't take it."

"You can tell him about me," Ryan said, "and about the safe house. Tell him Cat and Megan and I will meet him there tomorrow."

"He'll be fit to be tied once he finds out the truth," Mr. Mac warned.

Ryan nodded. "I'm hoping by this time tomorrow we'll have Megan back safe, so there's no need to worry him."

Mrs. Mac stood and switched off the coffeemaker. "We can drive Gabe to your safe house ourselves. No need to involve Mr. Brewster."

Tears flooded Cat's eyes at the down-to-earth goodness of her neighbors. "It will be a relief to know that Dad, at least, is safe."

"When you get to town," Ryan said, "could you place a call for me?"

Mr. Mac looked at him through narrowed eyes. "You think these Righteous Sword devils have tapped our phone?"

"I don't want to take that chance." Ryan pulled a pencil from his pocket, grabbed a paper napkin and printed a number on it. "This is Colonel Wentworth's private line. Tell him what's happened here tonight."

"Where can he get in touch with you?" Mr. Mac asked.

"We'll be at the ranch," Ryan said. "We'll wait there in case the kidnappers try to get in touch with us. But that phone may be tapped, too. The colonel will have to use his own judgment. Just tell him I'm counting on him to help me get my daughter back."

Mrs. Mac closed her arms around Cat in a warm hug. "Stay safe, Catherine. We'll look after your father. And we'll pray for Megan's safe return."

Numb with despair, Cat allowed Ryan to lead her to the car.

IN THE DIM LIGHT of the SUV, Ryan glanced at Cat, who hadn't moved or spoken since they left the MacIntosh place. His fear for Megan gnawed at him, and Cat's obvious pain broke his heart. "I'm sorry."

"What?" The look she gave him was stunned, as if she didn't know who or where she was.

"I should never have come back. None of this would have happened if I'd just told Wentworth no." Guilt ate at him like acid. His presence had caused his daughter's kidnapping and placed Cat at risk. He was too late to protect Megan, although he'd do everything in his power to get her back, but he could still save Cat. "It's not too late for you to go with Mr. and Mrs. Mac. I can take you back to them."

As if snapping out of a trance, she shook her head. "I'm not leaving Megan."

"We could be driving straight into a trap."

Her eyes flashed like blue fire. "Do you think I care what happens to me when those animals have my baby?"

"We can't help Megan if we're dead."

She couldn't deny the truth of that. "So how do we stay alive?"

"Do you still have that gun in the glove box?"

She reached over, opened the compartment and removed the gun. She offered it to him.

Ryan shook his head. "You keep it. We'll be most vulnerable when we return to the house. They might be waiting for us."

"Then why are we going back there?"

"I'm guessing that's where they'll try to contact us."

"To demand a ransom?"

Racked by guilt, he couldn't face her. He kept his attention on the road, where thick fog was swiftly obscuring the highway. "You know what they want."

"Us."

He nodded, reached over and squeezed her hand. "But they're not going to get us. We'll take their call and listen to their instructions. There are millions of acres of national forest out there, and the terrorists could be anywhere. So we have to figure out where they're hiding before we can rescue Megan."

"We will get her back, won't we?" Cat's voice broke on the question, and Ryan cursed himself again for what he'd done to her and his daughter.

"Or die trying," he promised.

Cat sat huddled in her seat, her jacket pulled tight around her, her eyes glazed as if in shock. More than anything, he wanted to stop the car and hold her. To reassure her that they'd find Megan. But he knew too well the chances of recovering his daughter alive and unharmed were slim. And he didn't dare express his fears to Cat. She was barely keeping hold of her sanity as it was.

In the thickening fog, the drive to High Valley took three times longer than usual, and every minute was agony. Ryan's arms and shoulders ached from tension as he gripped the wheel, and his efforts to see through the soupy mist had created a pounding headache. Worse than his physical discomfort, though, was the pain in his heart. The empty child carrier in the back seat reproached him, and a mental image of Megan, laughing and smiling, patting his face with her chubby hands, made him want to weep with fear for her and rage at her captors.

Cat hadn't blamed him, not once, but he wouldn't fault her if she hated him.

He hated himself.

Even if they were successful in retrieving Megan unharmed and escaping to the safe house, Cat, Megan and Gabe would never be safe until every member of Righteous Sword was apprehended. As slippery as the terrorist cell had been so far, capturing all of them any time soon seemed unlikely. However things played out, the situation would be lose–lose for the Ericksons. And equally bad for Ryan.

Anger boiled within him. The terrorists hadn't

killed him—not yet, at least—but they'd effectively killed his dreams. How could he and Cat and Megan ever hope to become a family when Ryan's return had placed them in constant danger and driven them from their home?

The open gate to High Valley loomed out of the fog, and Ryan breathed a sigh of relief. For the last few miles, his visibility had been so severely restricted, he'd had to inch his way forward to keep from plunging off the side of the mountain. He eased the vehicle through the gate and stopped.

Realizing they needed a plan, he shook off his self-pity and made himself think.

"We can't just waltz into the ranch," Ryan told her. "We have to make certain no one's waiting for us."

"How?"

"The fog will help conceal my approach. I'll park the car away from the house and sneak up without being seen."

He started the car slowly up the drive and strained to recognize landmarks in the shrouding mist. Before he reached the final bend in the road, he pulled onto the shoulder and stopped again. "I can't go any farther without the headlights announcing our arrival. And it's too foggy to drive in the dark."

Cat reached for the door handle. "We can follow the drive on foot."

With a hand on her shoulder, he stopped her. "You're staying here."

"I have my gun—"

"Let me check out the house first, then I'll come back for you."

"But you might need help. And you're not armed."

"If it's a trap, I don't want both of us walking into it. Once I've gone, curl up on the floor where you're hidden and wait. If I'm not back in an hour, take the car and go for the sheriff."

"No—"

He stopped her protests by pulling her into his arms and kissing her, savoring the taste of her and her honeysuckle scent, the warmth and weight of her in his arms. With regret, he drew back and cradled her face in his hands. "For Megan's sake, Cat, stay here and wait."

She nodded, her eyes dark and wide in the gloom. "What if someone besides you comes?"

"Kill them."

He took the house key from the ring, replaced the car key in the ignition, then slid from the car and quietly shut the door. The thunk of the electronic locks engaging reassured him that Cat was safely inside.

Using the edge of the gravel drive as his guide, Ryan crept toward the house, stopping every now and then to listen. He could hear no sounds except the moisture dripping from the plants and fence posts that lined the roadbed.

After fifteen excruciating minutes, he could finally discern the dark bulk of the house lifting out of the fog. No vehicle was parked out front, but he hadn't expected one. If the members of Righteous Sword were waiting, he was certain they were well hidden.

Instead of going straight to the front door, he circled the house and picked his way through the inky blankness of the yard to the barn. Once inside, he found a flashlight on the tool bench near the door and searched the interior. Since the barn was windowless, the sweeping beams of light couldn't be seen from the house. Assured the barn held no threat, he flicked off the flashlight, tucked it in his jacket pocket and returned to the house.

After circling the house and listening at each window for sounds of any occupants, Ryan crept up the back steps, unlocked the door and felt his way through the kitchen, the dining room and into the front hall. From its rack by the front door, he took Gabe's Winchester, glad to be armed but aware the single-shot rifle would be meager defense against the lethal automatic weapons favored by the terrorists.

His thorough search of the downstairs found it unoccupied and eerily silent. Upstairs, the rooms were also deserted. He stopped in Gabe's room long enough to retrieve the handgun from its hiding place on the top shelf of the closet and tuck it into his belt. A check of his watch revealed that fifty minutes had passed since he'd left Cat at the car. He sprinted down the stairs and out the front door.

He ran as fast as he could down the gravel road, unconcerned by the noise of his feet on the gravel. The dark bulk of the vehicle loomed out of the darkness, and he rapped on the window.

"It's me, Ryan," he called.

He heard the sound of the locks disengaging and opened the passenger door. Cat stared at him from the floor, her face stained with tears, her eyes hollows of despair.

"The house?" she asked.

"It's empty. You can get up now."

"My muscles have cramped," she said. "I can't move."

He helped her from the floor and out of the car. "Walk around and shake your legs to get the circulation flowing."

With a hobbling gait, she circled the car once. "I'm okay now. Let's go."

Wincing with discomfort, she climbed into the car. Ryan started the engine, turned on the headlights and drove the remaining distance to the front of the house.

As they climbed from the car, he heard the telephone ringing.

"I'll get it," Cat cried and raced toward the porch.

Ryan followed close on her heels.

By the time they'd opened the front door, the ringing had stopped.

"Oh, no." Cat sank to a chair in the hallway beside the phone. "We've missed them."

Ryan felt his heart sink. If the terrorists thought he and Cat had abandoned Megan, what would they do to her?

"They'll call back," he insisted with more assurance than he felt.

Cat's expression brightened. She pointed to the answering machine where a red light blinked. "They've left a message."

"It might not be the terrorists."

"Who else could it be?"

"Gabe or the MacIntoshes."

They both stared at the machine, and Ryan could sense his reluctance to hear the message reflected in Cat. Shaking off his hesitation, he hit Play.

A harsh, unfamiliar voice sounded in the stillness. "We have the girl. If you want her back, wait for our next call. Do not contact the authorities or we will kill her."

Cat gazed at him, her eyes filled with terror. "He didn't give a clue to where they are. How can we find her?"

"We can't." He forced himself to appear calm for Cat's sake, when rage at the terrorists and fear for Megan made him want to break something. "We have to wait for their call."

She looked as if she was going to collapse. He strode to the front door, locked the dead bolt, then turned to her. "Wait in the living room. I'm going to make coffee, then I'll join you there."

With a dazed nod, she pushed to her feet and walked into the other room. Ryan hurried into the kitchen, filled the coffeepot and put a kettle on to boil. He found the chamomile tea he knew Cat sometimes used to help her sleep and placed a tea bag in a cup. He needed the coffee to stay awake and stand guard, but he hoped to coax Cat into sleeping. They would both need all their energy and resources to outwit the terrorists, and he was worried about Cat. Concern for Megan seemed to have drained the life from her. He prayed a few hours sleep would revive her.

When the tea and coffee were ready, he assembled a tray and carried it into the living room. Cat sat curled on one end of a sofa, staring into space as if she were catatonic. She roused enough to give him a weak smile of thanks when he handed her a mug of tea.

Ryan shifted the sofa where she was sitting so that it faced the door of the living room, placed the rifle within easy reach, then switched off all the lights and opened the curtains before he settled next to Cat in the darkness.

"Why are they waiting so long to call back?" she asked.

"The fog could be slowing them down. They may want to reach their hiding place before contacting us again."

"Or they could be coming here for us while we wait for them to call." There was no panic, only stoic acceptance in her voice.

"That's a possibility," he said. "But they might not chance the possibility that the law could be waiting here with us."

They drank their beverages in silence, ears attuned to the telephone in the hallway. Ryan placed their empty mugs on the coffee table, then pulled Cat into the circle of his arm.

"Try to sleep," he said. "I'll keep watch."

He didn't know whether the tea had relaxed her or

her fears had finally exhausted her, but within minutes, she had quieted her nervous fidgeting. A glance at her face, however, showed her eyes wide open, alert.

"Can't sleep?" he asked.

She shook her head.

Ryan shifted slightly to a more comfortable position. The only sounds besides Cat's breathing were the ticking of the grandfather clock in the hall and the water dripping from the eaves of the house. Soon, however, a stiff breeze rustled the shrubbery surrounding the house. While Ryan watched through the uncovered windows, the prevailing west wind scattered the heavy fog.

He filled his coffee cup from the carafe on the tray. And waited.

And waited.

The grandfather clock chimed three.

The beam of headlights slashing through the uncovered window and across the room alerted him to the arrival of a vehicle.

Ryan shoved to his feet, grabbed the rifle and went to the window. An unfamiliar pickup truck pulled up behind Cat's SUV and parked. Immediately, two men climbed out and started toward the house.

Heart pounding, Ryan hurried to Cat. "Get your gun," he whispered. "We have company."

Chapter Twelve

Tamping down her rising fear, Cat tried to gauge Ryan's expression in the dark room. "Is it them?"

"Don't know."

Through the open drapery, Cat could see two strangers climbing the porch steps. Fearing the terrorists had come for them—and with no sign of Megan—she attempted to wrap her mind around the probability that she was going to die. And without seeing her daughter again. Denial kicked in, and a blessed numbness coursed through her.

But when one of them pounded on the front door, she jumped in alarm.

"Lieutenant Christopher! Open up!"

Beside her, Ryan stiffened, gun at the ready, his muscles tensed for action.

"Who's there?" he called.

"Colonel Wentworth."

With a sigh of relief, Cat sank back to the sofa, but Ryan didn't move or relax.

"I need proof, sir," he yelled.

A stream of Arabic split the air. Cat's nerves tightened at the sound, and she raised her gun toward the door, but Ryan laughed and lowered his weapon.

"It's all right," he assured her. "It's the password phrase I was given at the Pentagon."

After flipping on the lights in the hallway, Ryan unbolted the front door. A stocky man with a grizzled buzz cut and a pugnacious face and a taller fellow with flaming red hair and ear-to-ear freckles entered the foyer.

"How did you get here so fast?" Ryan asked.

"We hopped a military jet to Great Falls as soon as we discovered someone had tagged your prints," the man who'd identified himself as Wentworth said. "We learned en route about the kidnapping. A chopper brought us from the base to the airfield at the Athens ranger station."

His fierce expression softened when he turned to her. "I'm sorry about your daughter, Ms. Erickson. We'll do everything in our power to get her back safely."

The red-haired man nodded. "I'm Special Agent Jeff Bathurst, head of the FBI antiterrorist unit. I've brought a crack assault team—"

"No!" Cat felt the blood leave her head. "They'll kill Megan if they know you're here."

Ryan slid a consoling arm around her shoulders and guided her into the living room. The new arrivals followed. Ryan settled her on the sofa and turned on the lights, and Wentworth and Bathurst closed the curtains.

Bathurst sat across from Cat and leaned toward her.

"My team has gathered at the campgrounds south of here. They'll use that as a staging area for this operation. However, even to the most trained observer, they'll appear simply as hikers and campers. We don't want to tip off the terrorists any more than you do."

"Have you had a ransom request?" Wentworth asked.

Ryan shook his head. "Just the name Righteous Sword on a note pinned to Megan's teddy bear and a telephone message affirming they've got her. They said they'd call back."

Wentworth scowled at him. "Why didn't you report to the safe house on the base as ordered?"

"We were on our way," Cat said, unable to keep the catch from her voice, "but when we stopped to pick up Megan at the neighbors, she was gone."

"Where's your father?" Wentworth asked.

"My neighbors are taking him to the safe house," Cat explained. "They picked him up at the hospital. The terrorists broke his arm when they searched the house."

Wentworth fixed an intimidating gaze on Ryan. "Don't suppose you've remembered anything yet?"

"Not a damn thing," Ryan said in exasperation.

"Too bad," Wentworth said. "That means we'll have to take you all to the safe house after we get the girl back. You'll remain there until all the terrorists are rounded up. Maybe once we catch this group, one of them will cop a plea and tell us where to find the others."

Cat listened in amazement to the burly colonel. Her

hopes soared because he'd expressed no reservations about retrieving Megan, but dismay filled her at the prospect of living in hiding indefinitely.

"What would happen to the ranch?" she asked.

"We'll assign an FBI team here to take care of things," Bathurst assured her, "and to make certain we've flushed all the members of Righteous Sword from this part of the country."

"If you could remember the name of the embassy traitor," Wentworth said, pressing Ryan hard, "that would go a long way toward rounding up these bastards."

Frustration etched Ryan's face, and Cat longed to put her arms around him.

"What do we do now?" she asked.

"We wait," Bathurst said. "My men have put a trace on your phone line. When the kidnapper calls, we'll be able to locate the caller and tail him."

"It'll be daylight soon," Wentworth said. "The call could come any minute."

Cat curled in the corner of the sofa and prayed for her daughter's safety, hoping her little girl's captors were treating her kindly, feeding her, keeping her warm and unafraid...

Ryan took the coffee carafe to the kitchen to brew a fresh pot, and Wentworth made two trips to his truck, returning each time with a large cardboard carton.

Bathurst pulled a topographical map of the area from his jacket, spread it over the coffee table and studied it.

"Have you done this often?" Cat asked him.

"This?"

"Rescued children from terrorist kidnappers."

Bathurst sat back and considered her with intelligent blue eyes and a sympathetic expression. "We've conducted raids against terrorists before, but never where children were involved."

"Then how can you be so certain you'll rescue Megan?"

"Because my team is the best in the world. They're trained for every scenario." Bathurst expressed his belief with confidence but without cockiness. "If my daughter was kidnapped, the group that's gathered at the campground now are the people I'd want going after her."

Ryan returned with fresh coffee and extra mugs. He filled Cat's cup first and handed it to her. "How are you holding up?"

The concern in his voice and the love shining in his eyes almost undid her, and she swallowed tears. Afraid to trust herself to speak, she simply nodded and sipped her coffee.

Wentworth accepted a cup. "Do you have a speakerphone?"

Cat shook her head.

The colonel set down his coffee and rummaged in one of the cardboard cartons. He withdrew a telephone and a tape recorder and placed them on the table beside Bathurst's map. Then he fished out a coil of telephone wire, plugged it into the speakerphone and ran it to the jack in the hallway.

"When the phone rings," Wentworth told Ryan, "just press that button."

The phone rang as he finished speaking, and Cat bolted upright, pulse racing. Ryan pressed the speaker button, and Wentworth depressed record on the tape recorder.

"Hello?" Ryan said.

"It's me, Mrs. Mac." The woman's pleasant voice filled the room. "Called to let you know we've delivered that package you wanted and will wait here for you to claim it."

"Thanks, Mrs. Mac," Ryan said. "We'll be in touch."

He broke the connection, and the colonel stopped and rewound the recorder.

"At least we know that Daddy's okay," Cat said.

"I intend to keep your entire family safe," Wentworth said without bluster. "You've lost too much to Righteous Sword already."

Ryan topped off everyone's coffee, and they settled down to wait for the call from Righteous Sword. Early morning light filtered through the closed curtains, and with agonizing slowness, the chiming of the grandfather clock marked the passing of each quarter hour. Finally, just as the clock finished striking six, the phone rang again.

Cat's heart thundered in her throat, and she clasped a throw pillow against her chest to keep her hands from shaking.

Wentworth started the recorder, and Ryan answered the phone.

"Listen hard, Christopher," the rough voice commanded, "because we're only saying this once. If you want your daughter back, you, the Erickson woman and her father go directly to Lookout Point. Now. Come alone and unarmed. If we see anyone else who even looks suspicious, we'll kill the girl."

"Let me speak to Megan."

"The girl's not with me."

"How do I know she's okay?"

"Come to Lookout Point and find out."

"Where's Lookout Point?"

Cat knew Ryan was stalling for the FBI to have time to trace the call. He'd been to Lookout Point. He and Mark hiked there every time they came home on leave.

"Find a map," the voice answered with a snarl. "But if you're not there within three hours, the girl is dead."

"We'll be there," Ryan said, but the caller had already hung up.

Cat fought against rising hysteria. "How can we take Daddy to them? He's in Great Falls."

"Don't worry, Ms. Erickson," Wentworth said with a smile. "I wouldn't let him go even if he were here."

Understanding glimmered in Ryan's eyes. "You're going to stand in for Gabe."

"That's right," the colonel said. "We're about the same age. I'll pull my hat low over my face and wear my arm in a sling."

"The perfect place," Bathurst added with a boyish grin, "to conceal a weapon."

"We have some logistics problems," Ryan said, with what Cat thought was classic understatement. Logistics nightmare was more accurate.

"We always do." Bathurst didn't seem concerned.

Ryan knelt beside the map on the coffee table. "Lookout Point is the highest spot on the forest. It's a rocky promontory right on the Montana-Idaho border."

Cat leaned over and stabbed the map with her finger. "Right here."

"They picked their spot well," Ryan explained. "An old lookout cabin sits on the end of the promontory with a three-hundred-and-sixty-degree view of the entire forest. It's surrounded on three sides by sheer rock cliffs over one hundred feet straight down. The only approach is along a windswept ridge with no tree cover."

"You can reach only within two miles of it by logging road," Cat added. "You have to go the rest of the way on foot."

Her heart ached at the thought. Had someone carried Megan up the steep slopes or had the little girl had to scramble on her own?

"And," Ryan said with a frown, "from the lookout, every switchback up the mountain below can be clearly seen. There's no way to sneak your team up that road. And they'll spot you coming from miles away if you try an aerial insertion."

"I'll get my team in there," Bathurst said, "but

we'll need to move now. We'll meet you on the mountain.''

Wentworth walked Bathurst to their truck, and Cat watched them conferring briefly before the special agent climbed in and roared away. The colonel returned to the house, went to one of his cartons and pulled out three bulky black items. He tossed one to Ryan, handed another to Cat and kept the third for himself.

"Kevlar vests," Wentworth explained. "Bulletproof. Put these on beneath your clothes, then get your jackets. We don't want to be late."

Cat didn't have to be persuaded to hurry. The sooner they left, the sooner she'd have her daughter back.

RYAN PARKED the SUV in a turnaround at the end of the logging road on Lookout Mountain and checked his watch. As anxious as he was to retrieve his daughter, they couldn't be too early. They had to give Bathurst's team time to arrive.

Wentworth had explained the assault plan on the way up the mountain. The scheme seemed doable. The tricky part would be keeping Cat and Megan out of the line of fire. Making sure they were safe would be his job. He'd gotten them into this mess. He intended to get them out. Unharmed.

Gazing through the windshield, Ryan could see the lookout in crisp detail against the clear Montana sky. The lower floor was a square concrete block building with a window on each side and one door. Inside, a staircase led to the top floor, a lookout tower with four walls of solid windows. He could barely make out a dark form inside.

"No sign of another vehicle," Wentworth observed. "They're obviously not planning their getaway down the road we just used."

Ryan nodded toward the trail leading up through the snow. "Those tracks are fresh. At least two or three people climbed that trail recently."

Cat stared at the rugged path strewn with rocks and snow, and tears glistened in her eyes. "Megan didn't have her shoes on. Only bedroom slippers."

"Someone carried her," Ryan assured her. "Otherwise, she would have slowed them down."

He didn't want to consider the possibility that Megan wasn't there. Or where she might be if she wasn't.

Wentworth checked his watch. "Ready?"

With a grim nod, Ryan opened the door and hopped out. When he helped Cat out, he held her for a moment and whispered in her ear. "Everything's going to be all right. Just remember what you're supposed to do."

She gazed at him with trusting blue eyes. "I'm ready."

His heart swelled with love and pride. Other women in the same situation would be having hysterics by now. Even though he could read her fear for Megan in the tremor in her voice, she gave no other sign of her terror as she squared her shoulders and started up the trail.

Wentworth adjusted the sling on his arm and followed her. Ryan brought up the rear.

The trail, a grueling climb at an angle that at times seemed almost perpendicular, presented a formidable obstacle for an older man with the use of only one arm. For the first several yards, while they were still visible to the man in the lookout tower, Ryan assisted Wentworth up the slope. As soon as they reached the cover of the trees, however, the athletic colonel was able to make the climb on his own.

For the next hour, they hiked in silence. The only sound besides the wind soughing through the evergreens was the occasional rattle of a loose rock skittering down the path and the labored wheeze of their breathing.

When they neared the top, they paused beneath the trees before stepping onto the exposed ridge that led to the lookout. Ryan couldn't help remembering Cat's anxious question on the ride up the mountain.

"What if they just open fire and mow us down on the ridge?" she'd asked.

"They won't," Wentworth said.

"How can you be so sure?"

"Because they want to know what Ryan knows and who he's told," the colonel replied. "Until they're satisfied he's told them everything they need to know, we're safe."

"And Megan, too?" Cat said.

"Megan's the bait they'll use to lure us into the cabin," the colonel had explained.

While they caught their breath after the arduous

climb, Wentworth adjusted the sling on his arm and repositioned the small twenty-five-caliber automatic he'd hidden in its folds. Ryan checked the commando knife concealed in his boot.

"When we step into the open," Wentworth said to Cat, "call to them. Tell them we're not coming any closer until you've seen your daughter and know she's okay."

Cat nodded.

"Lieutenant, let me lean on you. I'm supposed to be exhausted from making that climb one-handed."

"Yes, sir." In spite of the seriousness of their situation, Ryan had to suppress a smile. Never had he seen anyone looking less weary than the colonel. Wentworth wasn't even breathing hard.

"Let us go first," Ryan said to Cat. In case Wentworth was wrong about the terrorists wanting them alive, he wanted to be between her and the line of fire.

"Okay."

The exertion of the climb had reddened her cheeks, and the mountain wind had tangled her golden blond hair into appealing curls around her face. Her blue eyes sparkled, whether with anticipation at seeing Megan or anxiety, he couldn't tell. All he knew was that Cat had never looked more beautiful, and he had never loved her more than he did this minute.

With Wentworth leaning on Ryan's left arm, the men stepped out of the trees onto the exposed ridge that led to the lookout. Ryan eyed the silhouette of the man in the tower, who turned and watched their approach.

Good, Ryan thought, *keep looking this way.*

The door of the first-floor cabin swung open, and a man stepped out with a Russian assault rifle cradled in his arms.

Ryan and Wentworth halted.

"I want to see my daughter," Cat called to the man, but the stiff wind atop the ridge whipped her words away.

The man motioned with his rifle for them to keep coming, but neither Ryan nor Wentworth nor Cat moved.

"Show us the girl," Ryan shouted.

Another man appeared in the doorway with Megan in his arms.

"Mommy!" she cried.

"Hi, sweetie," Cat called, her voice amazingly steady for someone who, Ryan knew, was scared out of her mind for her daughter's sake. "We've come to take you home."

"Now we know she's okay," Ryan whispered to Wentworth. He experienced a wave of relief so strong he had to lock his knees to keep them from buckling beneath him.

"And that there are at least three men altogether," the colonel muttered under his breath.

The man with the assault rifle motioned them forward again, and this time, the trio on the ridge bent into the wind and tramped toward the building.

When they were within a few feet of the cabin,

Megan wiggled so fiercely in the man's grip, he lost his grasp on her. She landed on her feet and flew across the rocky escarpment into Cat's arms.

"Search them," the man with the gun ordered his partner.

Suddenly the clatter of machine-gun fire and the shattering of glass in the tower above them split the stillness on the ridge.

From that moment on, for Ryan everything seemed to move in slow motion. Cat shoved Megan to the ground and threw herself over her daughter.

The man with the rifle glanced toward the broken windows of the lookout. The terrorist in the tower had disappeared. Wentworth used those precious seconds to draw his gun and drill a shot through the gunman's forehead. He fell backward and lay still.

The man who'd held Megan fumbled in his coat for his weapon just long enough for Ryan to pull his knife from his boot and jump him. Ryan wrestled the man to the ground and held the knife to his throat. "Don't move."

With automatic weapons at the ready, Bathurst and four members of his FBI team burst around the corners of the building. They had climbed the rock face for the assault on the tower and timed their arrival perfectly. The special agent waved two of his men inside.

"Secure the tower," he ordered, then tossed Ryan a pair of handcuffs and trained his gun on the captive until Ryan could cuff him. As soon as his prisoner was secure, Ryan grabbed the blanket Megan had dropped in her rush to her mother and covered the body of the terrorist Wentworth had killed.

He hurried to Cat, who had risen to her feet and was checking Megan for injuries.

His daughter broke into a huge smile. "Hi, Trace."

"You okay, short stuff?"

Megan nodded, but her expression sobered. "They were bad men. I wanted to go home. They wouldn't let me."

Cat hugged Megan and gazed at Ryan over their daughter's head. "It's okay, sweetie. We can go home now."

"Are you all right?" he asked Cat.

Her smile was as dazzling as the sun reflecting off the surrounding snow. "I'm fine."

Bathurst approached. "They had a truck and driver waiting at the bottom of the cliff and rappelling equipment at the top to use to escape. We captured their driver. He's the one who placed the telephone call."

"I wanna go home," Megan said.

"I'm afraid you won't be going home just yet." Wentworth stood beside them.

"Why not?" Cat asked.

Ryan felt a sinking in his stomach. He knew what the colonel was about to say.

"We have choppers coming to fly you to Great Falls," Wentworth announced. "You'll be staying at the safe house on the base for a while."

Cat frowned. "How long?"

Wentworth shrugged. "Until we round up the rest of Righteous Sword."

"But the ranch—"

"Don't worry." Bathurst had joined them. "I'll put a team in place to take care of things while you're gone."

The colonel and special agent returned to the lookout. Cat sat on a boulder and pulled Megan onto her lap, and Ryan removed his jacket and wrapped it around his daughter.

"Where are we going, Mommy?" Megan asked.

"To visit Grandpa," Ryan said. "He's in Great Falls."

His answer seemed to mollify Megan's concerns, but Cat gazed at him with questions in her eyes. Ryan placed his arm around her and pulled her close, but he couldn't tell her what she needed to hear. If Wentworth and Bathurst's teams couldn't ferret out the remainder of the terrorist cell, none of them would ever be safe at High Valley Ranch again.

LATE THAT NIGHT, Ryan sat in front of the fireplace in the safe house. The choppers had plucked them off the mountaintop, returned them to the ranch to gather their clothes, then flown them to the base at Great Falls.

Megan had been ecstatic through the entire trip, leaning toward the Plexiglas bubble for a better look at the mountains below. Unlike Megan, Cat had been a white-knuckle flyer who'd been happy to place her feet on solid ground again.

Gabe had been waiting for them at the house when they arrived. After putting Megan to bed for a nap, Cat had joined the men in the living room while Ryan told Gabe the entire story of his amnesia, the fake identity and the kidnapping attempt by Righteous Sword. His gut had churned with guilt and sorrow at the old man's expression when Gabe had digested the fact that he and his family might be in hiding for a long, long time.

"We can't stay on this base forever," Gabe said.

"If the search goes on too long," Ryan explained, "the government will place us in the witness protection program."

Gabe's eyes had filled with pain. "You mean new identities?"

Ryan nodded. "And a new location."

"But the ranch has been in our family for five generations," Cat cried. "We can't just walk away from it."

Gabe had reached for his daughter's hand. "We can if it means staying alive."

Remembering, Ryan was assaulted by fresh regret and anger. If he could only remember those last ten days before the bombing, he could point the investigators toward the traitor in the embassy. That man could hold the key to uncovering the rest of the cell.

He lay his head against the back of the couch and closed his eyes. The harder he tried to remember, the less he seemed to recall. But he had to do something. Although he knew Cat and Gabe were rejoicing at his miraculous return from the dead, he could gauge as well the grief they felt at being torn from their home and the land they loved.

Ryan breathed deeply and forced himself to relax. In his mind, he pictured the last memories he held of the days before the bombing. If he could only go forward another day or two...

A sudden weight landed on his stomach and shattered his concentration. Opening his eyes, he faced Megan, sitting on his lap. Cat stood behind her, watching them both.

"I came to tell you good-night," Megan said.

Her hair was still damp from her bath, and she looked adorable in her pink flannel gown. He ached at the sight of her, knowing the kind of life to which his amnesia had condemned her.

"Good night, short stuff. Do I get a kiss?"

She threw her chubby arms around his neck and kissed his lips. His arms tightened around his daughter, and he fought tears, recalling how close he'd come to losing her.

Megan drew back and studied his face. "Are you crying, Trace?"

He wiped his eyes with the back of his hand. "Must be the smoke from the fireplace."

Megan was fiddling with the collar of his shirt. "You lost a button. Mommy can get you a new one, can't you, Mommy."

Megan's observation triggered his recall of Marc's last words, and they replayed in Ryan's mind.

Did Ryan hit the button?

But Marc had been dying, his speech slurred. He

wasn't talking about buttons at all! Ryan hugged Megan and handed her to her mother. "I have to call Wentworth."

"What's wrong?" Cat asked.

Ryan couldn't help grinning. "Nothing's wrong. I have my memory back. You misunderstood Marc's last question about me. He wasn't talking about a button. He wanted to know if I got Derrick Hutton, the traitor in the embassy."

For the first time since their arrival in Great Falls, Cat's face lighted with hope. "You call Wentworth. I'll put Megan to bed."

When she returned a few minutes later, Ryan took her in his arms. "I gave Wentworth Hutton's name. He and Bathurst are on his trail."

She leaned back in his arms and gazed at him. "Then everything's going to be all right?"

"I can't guarantee it," he said honestly, "but there's a good chance we'll be home by Christmas."

Her smile warmed him. "What more could a woman want?"

"I have a few ideas," he said with a grin, "and they don't have to wait until December."

Epilogue

Cat stood on the front porch, watching the moon rise over the Cabinet Mountains. Even though it was a late October night, the weather was mild. Yesterday had been mild, too, a perfect Indian summer day. A perfect day for a wedding.

She and Ryan had been married in her mother's perennial garden at the ranch. Friends and neighbors from Athens and all over the valley had gathered to join in the celebration.

The screen door creaked, and in a moment, she felt Ryan slide his arms around her and draw her against him. His chin rested on the top of her head.

"Having second thoughts, Mrs. Christopher?"

"I'm just remembering what a wonderful wedding it was. I'm glad we were home in time to hold it outdoors."

"You can thank Derrick Hutton for that."

"That traitor?" She'd been so busy with plans for the wedding, she hadn't had time to catch up on the particulars of Hutton's capture.

"His attention to details," Ryan said, "is what

kept his group undiscovered for so long, but in the long run, it was also his undoing. As soon as Wentworth and Bathurst located him, they also found precise records of every member of the cell, their location and all their activities. That's why they caught them all so quickly.''

Cat shuddered. "Would Righteous Sword really have used suicide troops to pilot those boats filled with explosives into the Norfolk shipyards?''

"Hutton was ruthless. Wentworth caught them just in time.''

"But Hutton is an American. Why did he ally himself with Middle Eastern terrorists?''

"The man had a vendetta against the United States government. Some problem with his parents' business. His parents committed suicide as a result, and Hutton blamed America.''

Cat shook her head. "Hutton's bitterness caused all that death and destruction.''

"He won't bother us again, thank God. And neither will Snake Larson.''

"What's happened to Snake?''

"Gabe brought the news back from town this morning. Snake pleaded guilty to second-degree murder. Killed a man in a bar fight in Eureka. He'll spend the rest of his life in prison.''

When she shivered at the news, Ryan tightened his arms around her. "Let's talk about something else.''

Cat was happy to oblige. "Did you notice Todd Brewster at the wedding yesterday?''

"He seemed extremely cheerful, considering the

woman he wanted for his wife was marrying someone else."

Cat smiled. "You can thank Joyce Carruthers, the new home-economics teacher, for his happiness. I noticed how they sat together at supper and danced every dance with each other."

"Speaking of happy," Ryan added, "your dad seems to be on cloud nine."

"He has his ranch back and you to help him with it. I was so worried about him after Marc died, but he's rallying now. He's putting on weight, and the spring's back in his step. He'll never get over missing Marc, but he's coping better."

"Megan helps. She brightens all our lives." The pride in Ryan's voice was unmistakable.

"She's glad to have her father back." Cat paused and turned to face him. "But she's says there's still someone missing."

Ryan frowned. "Who?"

"She wants a baby brother."

His frown dissolved into a warm grin. "That could be arranged."

"On one condition," Cat teased.

Ryan raised an eyebrow.

"We have to agree on a name first."

"That doesn't sound like an insurmountable task," he said.

"Even if I want to name him after a man I once loved?"

Ryan narrowed his eyes. "What man is that?"

Cat grinned. "I want to call him Trace Gallagher."

"Trace Gallagher Christopher?" Ryan laughed. "That's some handle for a little boy."

"We'll shorten it to T.G. Or how about Tiger as a nickname?"

"Whatever you want," Ryan said agreeably, "but I'm ready for the next step."

"Decorating the nursery?" she asked with a twinkle in her eye.

His eyes burned with love as he lowered his head toward hers. "You know exactly what I'm talking about. Come to bed."

She slid her arms around his neck and arched on tiptoe for his kiss. "I thought you'd never ask."

Is he tall, dark and handsome...
Or tall, dark and *dangerous?*

Men of Mystery

Three full-length novels of romantic suspense from reader favorite

GAYLE WILSON

Gayle Wilson "has a good ear for dialogue and a knack for characterization that draws the reader into the story."
—*New York Times* bestselling author Linda Howard

**Look for it in June 2002—
wherever books are sold.**

HARLEQUIN®
Makes any time special ®

Three masters of the romantic suspense genre come together in this special Collector's Edition!

Unveiled

NEW YORK TIMES BESTSELLING AUTHORS

TESS GERRITSEN
STELLA CAMERON

And Harlequin Intrigue® author

AMANDA STEVENS

Nail-biting mystery...heart-pounding sensuality...and the temptation of the unknown come together in one magnificent trade-size volume. These three talented authors bring stories that will give you thrills *and* chills like never before!

Coming to your favorite retail outlet in August 2002.

Nail-biting mystery…
Sensuous passion…
Heart-racing excitement…
And a touch of the unknown!

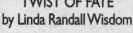

DREAMSCAPES...

four captivating paranormal romances promising all
of this—and more!

Take a walk on
the dark side with:

**THE PIRATE AND
HIS LADY**
by Margaret St. George

TWIST OF FATE
by Linda Randall Wisdom

THE RAVEN MASTER
by Diana Whitney

BURNING TIMES
by Evelyn Vaughn
Book 2 of The Circle

*Coming to a store near you
in June 2002.*

Where love comes alive™

Visit Silhouette at www.eHarlequin.com   RCDREAM7

Princes...Princesses...
London Castles...New York Mansions...
To live the life of a royal!

In 2002, Harlequin Books lets you escape to a world of royalty with these royally themed titles:

Temptation:
January 2002—*A Prince of a Guy* (#861)
February 2002—*A Noble Pursuit* (#865)

American Romance:
The Carradignes: American Royalty (Editorially linked series)
March 2002—*The Improperly Pregnant Princess* (#913)
April 2002—*The Unlawfully Wedded Princess* (#917)
May 2002—*The Simply Scandalous Princess* (#921)
November 2002—*The Inconveniently Engaged Prince* (#945)

Intrigue:
The Carradignes: A Royal Mystery (Editorially linked series)
June 2002—*The Duke's Covert Mission* (#666)

Chicago Confidential
September 2002—*Prince Under Cover* (#678)

The Crown Affair
October 2002—*Royal Target* (#682)
November 2002—*Royal Ransom* (#686)
December 2002—*Royal Pursuit* (#690)

Harlequin Romance:
June 2002—*His Majesty's Marriage* (#3703)
July 2002—*The Prince's Proposal* (#3709)

Harlequin Presents:
August 2002—*Society Weddings* (#2268)
September 2002—*The Prince's Pleasure* (#2274)

Duets:
September 2002—*Once Upon a Tiara/Henry Ever After* (#83)
October 2002—*Natalia's Story/Andrea's Story* (#85)

Celebrate a year of royalty with Harlequin Books!

Available at your favorite retail outlet.

HARLEQUIN®
Makes any time special ®

HSROY02

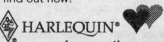